Can You Keep a Secret?

Other titles by Sandra Glover

Can You Keep a Secret?

Sandra Glover

Andersen Press • London

First published in 2002 by
Andersen Press Limited,
20 Vauxhall Bridge Road, London SW1V 2SA

British Library Cataloguing in Publication Data available
ISBN 0 86264 985 4

Typeset by FiSH Books, London WC1
Printed and bound in Great Britain by Mackays of Chatham Ltd.,
Chatham, Kent

Chapter 1

Karen stared at the glass on the floor. At the purple liquid staining her geography homework, dripping off the table and slowly seeping into the grey carpet.

She'd knocked over her drink in her dash to turn off the television, unable to bear what she'd just seen.

'Karen! What on earth . . . ?'

She turned to see her mother standing in the lounge doorway.

'Oh, for heaven's sake! You haven't spilt Ribena? Get a cloth quickly.'

When Karen returned with the cloth, her mother was still ranting on, giving the impression that she had, for the last few minutes, happily been lecturing an empty room.

'It's all over your homework, look. I told you not to do homework in the lounge. I suppose you were watching telly again?'

Karen nodded. She was too stunned by what she'd just seen to be bothered with explanations. She could have pointed out that she was only colouring a few maps. Nothing that required full concentration. That she was perfectly capable of watching at the same time. That she had, in fact, done both successfully.

Her mistake had been in not switching off the minute her programme ended. She'd let the early evening news run on, vaguely catching words like Europe, Ireland and

5

Chancellor of the Exchequer before something had really caught her attention. The lead item on the local news.

'You'll have to do the homework again. This is useless now,' said her mother, holding up two soggy pieces of paper and dropping them into the waste basket.

The homework! That was no problem. She had some spare maps, so half an hour would sort that out. But the news! If she was right about it, if it was what she thought, then half a lifetime wouldn't sort it out, let alone half an hour.

'Karen,' her mother said. 'Karen? Are you all right? You're shaking.'

'Cold,' said Karen. 'I'm a bit cold, that's all. I'll finish my work in my room. It's warmer up there.'

She picked up her bag and headed for her room. She couldn't tell her mother what she'd seen. Couldn't tell her anything. Not yet. Not until she'd calmed down.

Her mother would see it soon enough, of course. Later, on the ten o'clock news or in the evening paper. By tomorrow, everyone at school would know about it. Although not generally in the habit of discussing the finer points of news, they would certainly talk about this!

It wasn't the sort of thing that happened every day. Maybe a dozen cases a year, at most, across the whole country. Not the sort of thing you expected to turn up right here, in your own city, on your own doorstep, as it were.

Karen pushed open her bedroom door, dropped her bag and flopped onto the bed, her head ready to explode. What on earth was she going to do?

Whatever happened, whatever anybody said, she would have to be careful. She mustn't let anything show. No emotion. No sign that it was any more important to her than to anyone else. Not until she'd decided how much, if anything, she was going to tell. And who she would need to tell it to.

Secrets. She hated secrets. Even the nice kind bothered her. Like when you weren't supposed to let on what you'd bought Mum for her birthday. She was always worried that they'd slip out in an unguarded moment. More often secrets were the nasty kind. Zoë's kind. The ones you promised not to tell but knew, deep down, you should. And worse, much worse, were the third kind. Her kind. The really personal kind. The one you didn't ever want anybody to know.

And now? What now, when all the secrets flooded into her mind at once, drowning her brain, refusing to let her think rationally?

She got up, moved to her desk and tried to concentrate on the maps. Blot it all out. Her usual defence. But how could she concentrate? Seeing what she'd seen. Knowing what she knew.

The police had pleaded for witnesses. Begged anyone who had any information to come forward. So what was she waiting for? Her instinct was to pick up the phone. But what could she tell them? What did she really know? Nothing. It was guesswork. Circumstantial evidence, as the police might say. She was probably wrong. Over-reacting. Maybe it wasn't anything to do with Zoë at all.

'Calm down,' Karen told herself. 'Think!'

She began mechanically colouring her maps whilst considering her next move. Zoë. She couldn't do anything until she'd spoken to Zoë.

Strange to think that a year ago there had been no Zoë. Well, there had. There had been Zoë and there had been Karen. Completely oblivious to each other's existence. Leading separate lives, growing up in different parts of the country. Then, one night, a giant hand had reached out, snatched her up and dropped her right here in Zoë's city, Zoë's school, Zoë's class.

It hadn't really happened like that, of course. But sometimes it seemed that way. Easier to believe that some mischievous being had planned it all, than to accept that it was only a bizarre series of random coincidences which had brought them together.

Perhaps Mr Harrison was to blame, Karen thought, as she looked down at her map, with half of the English Channel coloured red. She screwed it up and began again.

Mr Harrison had owned the small but successful engineering company in Manchester where her father had worked. Mr Harrison had sold his firm to a much larger company. Within a year they had merged it with another site, making half the workers, including her dad, redundant.

There had followed an awful six months, with her dad applying for jobs, going to interviews, being turned down, and getting depressed. At first he had applied only for jobs in and around Manchester. As he became

8

desperate he applied further afield. Birmingham, London and even to a company which wanted workers for a five-year contract in China.

So, it could have been worse. Possibly. When he got this job in Leeds, they had greeted it like a jackpot win on the Lottery.

'It's only the other side of the Pennines,' her dad had said. 'We might not even have to move. I can commute.'

Pennines. Karen studied her map. Manchester and Leeds looked no distance at all but in reality it hadn't been that simple. Nothing ever was.

Dad had started his job last February. For the first few months he had tried commuting. But driving twice a day up and down the motorway in heavy traffic and bad weather, combined with the long hours he was working, was making him ill. At the beginning of April, a year ago to this very day, they put their house up for sale.

'It won't be too bad,' her mum had said. 'I'll easily get another job and if we can move by the summer, Karen will be able to start Year Ten in a new school.'

Again, not as easy as it sounded. In May they had found a house they liked, chosen a school and picked some GCSE courses. Then the owners of the house had decided not to sell after all.

So maybe they were to blame. If they'd kept to the deal, she'd have gone to that school. Not this one. Not Zoë's school. As it was, they were lucky, Mum said. They found another house. Vacant possession. The owner had recently died and the relatives were anxious for a quick sale.

'Spooky,' Karen had said. 'Hope he's not still hanging around.'

But her problems, as it turned out, had nothing to do with ghosts.

The house was on the opposite side of the city to their original choice. They had moved on August 29th. A week later, they'd turned up at the local comprehensive, seen the Head, hastily chosen some courses, beetled off to buy a uniform and that was that.

Barely time to panic about new classmates, strange teachers, different rules and finding your way round. All the things you'd usually panic about on your first day.

In fact, it had been remarkably easy at first. Mrs Wilson, her form tutor, was the jolly, motherly type who went to great pains to make sure Karen settled in.

'Shaheen and Paula will look after you,' she announced. 'You're in their groups for most subjects.'

This wasn't entirely coincidence. Shaheen, Paula and Karen had chosen similar options because they had similar interests. Geography in preference to history. Food technology from the practical options. They were roughly of the same ability. Top sets for everything. And though Shaheen and Paula had been friends since junior school, Karen had no problem fitting in. The pair became a trio.

Most of the Year 10s were easy enough to get along with. There were five rather loud, obnoxious lads in her tutor group, but as they were in bottom sets, she didn't see much of them. Of the girls, only two were hostile. Tracy and Zoë. The dreadful duo.

They looked a little older than the rest, probably because they wore more make-up and took liberties with the uniform. They sat at the back of the class, giggling when she spoke, making stupid comments about her accent.

'Don't take no notice,' Shaheen had said, the first time it happened. 'If you don't let on you're bothered, they'll stop. They have a go at everybody, those two. If it wasn't your accent, it'd be the colour of your skin or your hair or something. They think there's only two perfect people in this world. And that's them.'

'Perfect pains, more like,' Paula had said. 'Tracy reckons she's right superior since she did that bit of modelling. She used to be in top sets, you know. But she says she doesn't need to work any more 'cos she's going to be a professional model. Dream on, eh?'

Maybe it wasn't a dream, Karen had thought. Tracy had seemed, to her untrained eye, to have the right attributes. Tall, with blonde hair, enormous green eyes and a figure as thin and straight as the sticks of celery she nibbled at lunch time.

'And Zoë,' Paula explained, 'deliberately mucked up her exams so she'd get moved down to middle sets with Tracy. Idiot. I mean, she's not going to be a model, is she?'

Not that Zoë wasn't pretty. Deep brown eyes, masses of dark hair falling round her shoulders and an easy smile which could mislead you into thinking she was pleasant. But she was small with an already full figure, verging on plump.

11

'She's going to be fat, like her mum,' Paula had added knowledgeably.

'And just as idle,' said Shaheen. 'Her mum worked with my mum for a bit, four years ago, just after Zoë's dad left. But she didn't stick it long. She was always turning up late, taking time off...I think they sacked her in the end. Hasn't worked since, as far as I know.'

Karen had barely listened. It didn't concern her. There was no way she was ever going to have anything to do with that pair. Or so she thought. In tutor time Tracy and Zoë sat well away from her. At break they scuttled off behind the arts block to smoke. They went out most lunch times, getting back late, if at all. Every week they were in detentions which they rarely bothered to turn up for.

'They're getting worse, they are,' Shaheen said, shortly after the October half term, when Tracy threw a hockey stick at the PE teacher for daring to suggest that she might like to join in a games lesson.

Tracy. The trouble really started with Tracy and that dreadful business at the end of last term.

Karen shook her head, not wanting to dwell on it. She held up her map. Not bad, under the circumstances. Not perfect. At one time she'd have worked on it a bit more. As it was, she threw it aside and started on the second one.

She wasn't so keen on geography these days. Not since the New Year, when the sets had been merged and they'd ended up with a class of thirty-five. Maybe it would be better after Easter when the new teacher came and the groups could be split again.

She wondered what had happened to the old teacher. To Mr Parsons. He wouldn't have got another job. Not in teaching, surely? Not after what Tracy and Zoë had done.

Chapter 2

Christmas had been the beginning of the end. For Karen and for poor Mr Parsons. When Karen had started at the school in September, there had been three geography sets. The Head of Department took the top set, the Deputy Headmaster took the bottom set, to keep them in order as much as to try to teach them anything, and Mr Parsons had the middle group.

He had been at the school less than a year and Karen knew him only by sight. Young, quite tall, thin and with a dark beard which covered a fair proportion of the spots which plagued his face. Shaheen and Paula, though they had never been taught by him, knew a little more. He'd joined the school straight from college, which accounted for his youth. He was single, which made him a target for a variety of unsavoury, almost certainly untrue, rumours. He played the guitar and ran the debating society, which made him a favourite with the sixth form. He was nice. And that, of course, was his major problem.

Within a month of his arrival, even the little Year 7s had sussed that nice Mr Parsons let you off homework. Nice Mr Parsons didn't shout if you were late for lessons or make a fuss if you chatted to your mates. He accepted endless excuses and talked to you quietly about your imaginary problems.

By the time Mr Parsons had realized that nice probably

wasn't such a good idea in a teacher, most of his classes had deteriorated into near riots. Best were his A-level students and worst, by far, was middle set, Year 10. Tracy and Zoë's group.

Brighter students became aware that, this year, something was being done to help Mr Parsons. Senior teachers dropped into his lessons with increasing frequency. He had started to insist that pupils stayed in their seats for at least part of the lesson. Who knows? He might have succeeded. Given time.

The couple of weeks before Christmas are never the best time of year for a teacher, particularly one with problems. Lessons disrupted by last-minute choir practices. Concentration, of even the keenest pupil, impaired by garish decorations dangling from the class-room ceiling and the thought of a new computer peeping out of their Christmas stocking. Junior hormones running riot in anticipation of wild parties. Bodies fuelled, at best by a surge of adrenaline and surfeit of mince pies, at worst by the alcohol consumed behind the arts block.

Tracy had been the first to feel the Christmas spirit, smuggling into school the bottles of French wine, German beer and Polish vodka her father had brought back from his latest trips. Tracy's dad drove coaches. European tours, mostly. And there were always so many bottles in the house, he never knew what was missing.

Not that Karen knew anything about Tracy's dad or the alcohol, at the time. All that she knew had been pieced together later.

You didn't have to have much imagination to work out what had happened, though. She could see them all now. Tracy and Zoë's usual hangers-on — boys mostly. One standing guard, the rest lighting cigarettes, swigging beer and shoving the empty bottles in the gap between the arts block and the school's high security fence.

Zoë and Tracy eventually getting bored. They didn't like boys their own age. They were after better sport. Several people had noticed them, that lunch time, bounding back into school, early for once.

They had headed for the lower hall, where some Year 7s had been putting up some extra decorations for their Christmas party. A few had cried when Tracy and Zoë ripped them down. One girl had been punched in the stomach but by the time she had reported it, Tracy and Zoë had gone, clutching some balloons and a sprig of mistletoe.

There were no actual witnesses to what happened next, Karen mused, putting her maps into her folder. But it wasn't hard to guess. The only question was whether they had stumbled upon poor Mr Parsons by chance on their way to tutor group or deliberately headed for his room.

Either way, they found him there alone. Went in. Closed the door. Decided to have a bit of sport with the mistletoe, maybe.

Karen had always believed that he was pushing Tracy away when it happened. That she hurt herself when she fell against the desk, screamed and grabbed hold of him to stop her fall.

16

That was his story, when the Deputy Head, alerted by the scream, walked in and found them both sprawled out together on the floor, Zoë placidly looking on.

Their story was completely different. Sure, they had been drinking. Yes, they had engaged in a bit of fun down in the hall. But then, they had sobered up and decided to go quietly to registration. As they passed Mr Parsons' room, he had called them in. Made suggestions. Lewd comments about schoolgirl models. As they tried to leave, he'd made a grab at Tracy...

Although not known as the most truthful girls in the school, it was two against one. Their story against his. Not helped by the fact that Tracy had a bruised back and torn shirt.

It had been hushed up as much as possible. The details Karen had got from Zoë later. Much later. How Tracy's parents had threatened to go to the press. How the Head had panicked.

'I reckon,' Zoë had said, 'he was half glad of an excuse to get rid of Mr Parsons anyway. I mean, let's face it, he was useless.'

'Being a lousy teacher's one thing,' Karen had argued. 'But being sacked for *that*!'

'He wasn't sacked,' Zoë had claimed. 'He agreed to go. He resigned.'

Karen still didn't know whether that was true. Ninety per cent of what came out of Zoë's mouth was lies. You never got to the bottom of anything with Zoë.

Karen had asked time and time again, what had really

happened in that room.

'How should I know?' was Zoë's usual response. 'I was that drunk I can't remember. I haven't a clue.'

'That's not what you said at the time,' Karen would argue. 'You backed Tracy. Every word.'

'Yeah, well. You stick up for your mates, don't you?'

Not that it had done Zoë much good. Both girls had been suspended until the New Year, for the drinking and wrecking the hall, allegedly.

But, in January, Zoë had returned alone. Tracy's parents had taken her away from the school completely, claiming that Zoë was a bad influence on their daughter. Most people tended to think it was the other way round. There were all sorts of silly rumours about why Tracy might have left. She'd got a big modelling contract. She was pregnant. She was heavily into drugs. She'd eloped with Mr Parsons! But, for Karen, none of that was an issue. She didn't care what Tracy was up to.

The point, then, was that Tracy's departure opened up a whole new set of circumstances. Zoë, at the start of term, was a loose cannon meandering around looking for a target.

'Me,' said Karen aloud. 'But why me, of all people?'

She was so busy pondering, re-living this last dreadful year of her life, that she barely heard the bedroom door opening.

'Did you shout?' said her mother.

'No, er, well, I was sort of talking to myself, getting mad with the homework. That's all. I've done it now.'

'Oh, right,' said her mother. 'Your dad's home, you know. Are you coming down?'

'Yeah, sure,' said Karen, following her mother downstairs. At the bottom her mother paused.

'He's brought the evening paper.'

No big announcement there, Karen thought. Her father bought a paper every night on his way home. She waited for the inevitable.

'There's a story, on the front...'

If it hadn't been so serious Karen would have laughed. Whoever heard of a story on the front of a newspaper!

'I wondered if you'd seen it earlier on the news?'

'Yes, I saw it,' said Karen, her eyes immediately filling with tears.

'I thought so,' said her mother knowingly. 'Do you want to talk about it?'

'No,' she wanted to scream. 'No I don't.'

But it was too late. Her mother had already started. Not that it was much of a conversation. More a monologue. Her mother talking. Dad nodding, picking at his dinner, making the occasional comment. Karen listening. They were trying to help. She knew that. Trying to take away some of the pain. But they couldn't. Not this time.

They thought they had all the answers. Thought they knew why she was so upset. But they didn't. They didn't know one half of it. And there was no way she could enlighten them. Not yet. Not until she was sure herself.

Zoë. Zoë was the one she needed to talk to. She needed to speak to her now. Tonight. Why had she put it off for so long? Going on with her homework as though everything was normal. Was she scared? Scared of asking the questions? Scared of hearing the truth? Dead right she was.

'I need to phone Zoë,' she said, when she felt the conversation was over.

Ignoring the kitchen phone, she headed for the privacy of the lounge, pausing in the hall long enough to hear her parents' anxious whispers.

'I suppose it's natural,' her mother said, 'now she's getting older, for her to turn to her friends rather than us. It's just that I feel so helpless.'

'I'd feel better if it were any other friend,' her father said. 'I mean, for the past few months it's been all Zoë. Whatever happened to those nice girls? Paula and Shaheen?'

Karen dropped onto the floor in front of the coffee table where the phone sat, daring her to pick it up. She could have told her dad that nothing had happened to the nice girls. Paula and Shaheen were still around. They were still her friends. It was just that since Tracy had left, Zoë had sort of taken her over. Made her into her own private property.

How had she let it happen?

It had started in the second week of January. With nothing much to do in class since her best mate had left, Zoë had resorted to work. Her maths was restored to its former standard. She did well in a French test. She caught up with her English assignments during the lonely lunch hours, and some idiot teacher made a suggestion:

20

'I think Zoë could move back to top sets.'

The first Karen knew about it was when Zoë turned up to their French lesson. There were six tables of four people. And one table with only three. No choice. Zoë must sit with them.

The same in maths. Only one vacant seat. Guess where? Even in lessons where there was acres of space, Zoë fell into the habit of joining them. In tutor time she edged away from the boys at the back to sit with Karen. And she wasn't the sort of person you could tell to get lost. Besides, she wasn't too bad in class any more.

In fact, she had been really quiet, those first few weeks, hovering around with them at breaks but barely speaking.

'Probably doesn't reckon we're worth talking to,' Paula had said. 'I wonder why she bothers tagging along.'

''Cos no one else'll put up with her,' said Shaheen, adding for Karen's benefit, 'She's had a go at everyone at some time or other. I daren't even tell my mum she's latched onto us. I had right bother with her in Year Eight when her and Tracy were into their racist kick. I was throwing up every morning, I was so scared to come to school.'

'So what happened?' Karen had asked.

'Well, after all the hospital tests proved negative, some bright spark of a doctor caught on that it was psychological and it all sort of came out. My mum came up to school, had a word with the Head, who shoved the school's anti-racist policy under her nose and promised to sort it.'

'And did he?'

'He'd claim he did. They left me alone after that. But the truth was, it was coming to an end anyway. They'd got bored with Asians. Fat was the new target. It was Gemma's turn to sit crying in the stock cupboard. That was before Zoë started to put weight on herself. Fat's all right now. But they plagued Gemma right through Year Nine.'

'And didn't anybody ever say anything? I mean, you knew what it was like. Didn't you stick up for Gemma?'

'Get real,' Shaheen had snapped. 'I was just grateful to be left alone. I mean, Zoë on her own seems OK but when she was with Tracy – well, you saw what they were like. Even the Head backed down over poor Mr Parsons. He must have known they were lying through their teeth.'

Paula had been a target too. Earlier on, shortly after joining the school, when she had to have a brace to straighten her teeth. But she and Shaheen were prepared to forgive and forget. To give the new Zoë a chance.

Karen looked again at the phone. A saying about leopards not changing their spots sprang to mind. They'd all been conned, believing Zoë's calm phase to be a combination of missing Tracy and a genuine desire to make new friends. But there had been other reasons for Zoë's quiet abstraction. The spots had never really gone away.

Chapter 3

'Hi, it's Karen. Is Zoë there?'

The voice of Zoë's mother came back, sleepy and casual.

'In bed?' said Karen, looking at her watch. 'Not well. Yeah, I know she wasn't in school today but I thought . . . Couldn't she just come to the phone? No . . . back in school tomorrow. OK, it'll wait.'

It would have to. But for how long? Would Zoë really turn up to school tomorrow as though nothing had happened? If anything *had* happened. It was still possible, almost possible, that this had nothing to do with Zoë.

It wasn't unusual for Zoë to be away on a Monday. Zoë's three-day weekends were famous throughout the school. So the news story and Zoë's absence might be coincidence. Unlikely . . . but so much of Karen's life recently seemed to be governed by coincidence that one more would hardly make much difference.

Karen padded back upstairs. Ran a bath. Poured in half a bottle of foam and lay up to her neck in soap suds. It didn't help. She wondered if you could sue them under trade descriptions or something. The claims on the bottle, that this foam relieved tension, were clearly untrue. It wasn't relieving her tension.

Her mind was still working overtime, wondering whether she ought to phone the police. Knowing that she couldn't, until she was sure. And even then? Even if she was one hundred per cent certain. Hadn't she made a promise? Hadn't she promised not to tell?

'Idiot!' she told herself.

How had she allowed herself to get so involved?

She should have seen it coming. It wasn't Shaheen's fault. Or Paula's. It was only natural that, with them being mates from way back and both having been Zoë's victims in the past, they should stick together. Avoid being alone with Zoë. Getting too close.

It had all happened so gradually. Every time they were required to pair off for something it was Karen and Zoë. When Zoë needed a bit of help with work, it was Karen she turned to. On her birthday, it was Karen she asked round.

Until then, Karen had managed to avoid much contact with Zoë out of school. They didn't live close. They had different interests. Karen's evenings were taken up with swimming club, music lessons and homework. Her weekends with shopping, going back to visit friends in Manchester, going bowling or sometimes to parties. But they weren't the same ones Zoë went to, if she went anywhere at all these days.

Since her departure from school, Tracy had, allegedly, done a bit more modelling and was studying at home. The ban on seeing Zoë didn't seem to bother her too much. She had a new boyfriend. She had her own life to lead, as she curtly informed her old mate on the phone. But without Tracy to organize her social life, Zoë had none. As far as Karen could gather, Zoë's evenings were now spent watching telly with her mum and sometimes going down the pub with her at weekends.

Zoë had invited her places before but Karen had always had an excuse ready. Not so easy on somebody's birthday. And besides it had sounded harmless enough.

'Can you come round on Sunday? I'm not doing anything special 'cos Mum's bought us a new computer and can't afford a party or nothing. And it's no use askin' Dad for money. Even if I knew where he was, which I don't. So I thought you and me could pig out on some cake and stuff and get the computer set up.'

So that cold Sunday early in February, just two months ago, Karen's dad had dropped her off outside the terraced house in the narrow street where Zoë lived.

'Computer's in the spare bedroom, well – boxroom really,' Zoë had said. 'It's a right hole, this place, isn't it? We had to move when Dad left. He thinks he's a right hero 'cos he sends money every month, but him and his partner, as he so grandly calls her, live in a right smart flat.'

'I thought you didn't know where your dad was.'

'I don't,' she had said, without a moment's hesitation. 'Not now. They moved after Mum's last visit.'

Zoë had laughed. 'Mum got a bit worked up. Put a brick through the window when she left. So they haven't bothered mentioning their new address. But I'll wheedle it out of him next time he bothers to come and see me. He's forgotten my birthday, you know. Not so much as a flaming card. Would you believe that?'

Karen hadn't had time to answer. Zoë was already

opening packages, fiddling with wires, throwing the instruction book across the room in frustration.

'Twenty minutes, it says!' she had yelled. 'Set up your computer in twenty minutes. Twenty flaming years, more like. It'll be obsolete by the time I've figured out how to get the monitor out of the box. It's all wedged in, look.'

'Careful,' Karen had warned. 'You're going to break it.'

Together they had eased it out, and lifted it onto the desk.

'Look,' Karen had said, rescuing the instructions. 'It says connect the black wire to the monitor.'

'Which black wire? There's three that I can see.'

'Can't your mum help?'

Zoë had laughed. She laughed a lot, did Zoë. Even when it was obvious she was depressed or mad about something. Like laughing was a sort of defence mechanism, to stop something worse exploding inside. It got her into a lot of trouble at school.

'My mum?' Zoë had eventually repeated. 'My mum still thinks a mouse is something you leap on the table and scream at! She can't even programme the video. Thick as school custard, she is.'

'Zoë!' Karen had protested.

'Don't get your knickers in a twist. She is thick and she'd be the first to admit it. I get my brains from my dad. He'd have this sorted in no time, if he was here. Which he isn't. So it's you and me. Right?'

'OK,' Karen agreed.

'I didn't mean anything nasty about my mum,' Zoë

added, trying to ram a connection into what was clearly the wrong socket. 'We get on great, most of the time. She doesn't get on at me all the time like Dad used to do. Goes to extremes, he does. When he was here he was always on at me about doin' well at school and stuff. Now he doesn't even ask. Doesn't know I've moved back to top sets. Didn't even know I'd been moved down, now I come to think about it! Wait till he finds out about . . . well, it don't matter. He can't hardly say anything after what he's done.'

She had shut up then. Concentrated on the computer, leaving Karen with not the foggiest clue what she'd been on about. Miraculously, they'd got the computer set up. Tried out a few games. Made a poster. Then Zoë's mum had shouted to them.

They were peas in a pod, those two. You could pick them out as mother and daughter in any crowd.

'Get my looks from Mum,' Zoë had said proudly, when Karen mentioned the likeness. 'And my brains from my dad, like I said. Not a bad deal, eh?'

Her mum was a good cook too. She'd made her own quiche and pizza, as well as a cake for Zoë. Not that Zoë ate much of it. She picked at a bit of salad and had the tiniest wedge of cake, putting half of the rest in a bag for Karen to take home.

'She's like me,' said Zoë's mum, looking regretfully down at her thick thighs. 'Puts on weight just looking at food. She must do. She hardly eats anything at home. I expect she's gorging sweets and crisps at school.'

'You guessed,' said Zoë, smiling. 'I reckon they should

27

close that tuck shop. It's too much of a temptation. I can't walk past without having something.'

Karen had said nothing. She knew it wasn't true. She'd never seen Zoë in the shop. Never. Funny thing to lie about that. Her lies were the other way round. She told her mother she only spent a pound a week on sweets and snacks when it was more like a pound a day. If she confessed the truth, it would mean endless lectures about rotting teeth and cellulite.

Clearly not the sort of thing Zoë's mum worried about. After tea, she settled down in front of the television with a box of chocolates, sending the girls back to the computer with a large box of their own. Zoë ate only one but the downstairs box was empty when the time came for Karen to leave.

So the day itself hadn't been too bad, Karen thought, as she climbed out of the bath. At that point there had been so much about Zoë that didn't make sense. So much she didn't understand. There still was, in a way, even though she now knew the whole story... or most of it.

Karen decided against going back downstairs. Instead she got into bed, picked up a book and put it down again. Why bother reading? What was that saying? 'Truth is stranger than fiction.' It certainly was at the moment. No book could compete with what was going on in her own life. In Zoë's life. No problem could be more depressing than the one which confronted her. The one she would face tomorrow, when she saw Zoë – if Zoë was in school.

She wasn't, of course. Karen sat, mechanically answering her name as Mrs Wilson read out the register. No one commented on Zoë's absence. It was too common an occurrence. Even since January, with Tracy's departure, Zoë's new leaf-turning didn't exactly involve regular attendance.

Usually Karen saw it as a blessing. A Zoë-free day left her more time to spend with Paula and Shaheen. But not today. Today she didn't want to talk to anyone but Zoë.

Register over, they were supposed to get on with tutorial work. Filling in endless questionnaires about career plans, how you thought you were getting on at school and what sort of person you were.

Today nobody had time for questionnaires. They were all talking about the news. Even those who hadn't read the paper or switched on their radios quickly picked up the gist and felt qualified to comment.

'You heard about that baby then,' said one lad, starting it off, 'that was found outside the medical centre yesterday morning?'

Karen nodded, determined to show nothing more than casual curiosity.

'Well, my neighbour reckons she saw the box,' he added. 'On her way to work. About seven o'clock. Didn't do anything, 'cos she thought it was just an empty box which had blown onto the step.'

'Yeah, well,' said Paula. 'It's not the sort of thing you expect, is it? You read about these things but you don't ever think you'll come across it yourself. A few streets away from your school! I mean, chances are, this is someone local. Maybe even someone we know.'

'I wonder...' said one of the boys, staring pointedly at the girls.

'Not funny, Alan,' said Shaheen, hitting him across the head.

'Shaheen!' snapped Mrs Wilson, momentarily looking up from a pile of papers she was sorting out. 'What on earth are you doing? Leave him alone and get on.'

'Hey, I know!' whispered one of the girls. 'What about Tracy? She left school in a bit of a hurry, didn't she? Nobody's seen her around for a while. What if she's been hiding a bulge all this time?'

Tracy, Karen thought. They were getting close!

'Not the sort of thing you want with you on the catwalk, is it?' someone sneered. 'Here we have Tracy modelling the latest accessory.'

'I said it's not funny!' hissed Shaheen. 'So don't go spreading stupid rumours. It could be anybody. Someone from outside the area, even. But whoever it is, it's not something to joke about.'

Dead right there, thought Karen bitterly.

'Imagine what a state the poor mother must have been in,' Shaheen went on, 'to do something like that!'

'I don't know how anybody can!' said Paula. 'Did you see him with that nurse? He was so sweet! I mean, just what sort of person dumps their baby and walks away?'

Karen had heard enough. She jumped up, pushed past

30

Mrs Wilson's desk, darted outside, down the corridor, into the loo. Just in time. Crouching down, she regurgitated her breakfast, which had been eaten in haste, in order to get to school early to see Zoë.

Stupid. Stupid. Stupid. How had she even imagined Zoë would be there? Still, she wasn't as stupid as some. They were barking way up the wrong tree with Tracy. And not one of them realized the truth, when it was right under their noses! Nobody had connected Zoë's absence with the story they were all bleating about.

On the other hand, would *she* have guessed? Probably not. Not if it hadn't been for that Tuesday, just after Zoë's birthday.

'Karen. Karen. Are you all right?'

Mrs Wilson's voice came through the door.

'Er, yes, Miss. Sorry, Miss,' said Karen, appearing, blinking tears back from her eyes. 'I don't feel too well. Been sick. Bug, I expect.'

'Do you want to go home?'

'Er, no, I'll be OK . . . I think.'

'They've all gone to first lesson. Games, isn't it? Shall I write you a quick note?'

'No, thanks. I'll be OK now. Honest.'

She wasn't OK but right at that moment she'd have said anything to get rid of Mrs Wilson. She needed to be on her own, just for a few minutes, to get a grip.

Once she got to games, she'd be all right, she told herself. She liked games. She was one of the few Year 10 girls who did. She was good at games. Throwing yourself into a game of tennis or netball could take your mind off things. Usually. Today, though, might be tricky. She suspected that there hadn't yet been a game invented which could take her mind off Zoë and that baby.

Chapter 4

Karen walked into the changing room in a daze. Most of the girls were changed. Several hovered by the teacher, Mrs Platt. Some were clutching notes, others were busily making up excuses.

Karen walked past them into a cubicle and pulled the curtain. It was only then that she realized. No kit. It wasn't even in school. She'd left it at home this morning, when games kit was the last thing on her mind.

By the time she left the cubicle the queue had gone, the offending girls banished. Mrs Platt screeched at Karen the minute 'forgotten' was out of her mouth.

Mrs Platt had a system of dividing up the refusers. First in the queue were sent to the library, others to tidy out the games cupboard or to collect litter from the corridors. Late arrivals and people she didn't like got outdoor litter duty.

Karen picked up the black bin-liner and headed outside. It wasn't fair. She hardly ever cried off games. It had only happened once before. That Tuesday, just after Zoë's birthday, when Karen's kit had disappeared from the cloakroom only to reappear, miraculously, later in the day.

She realized now, of course, that Zoë had taken it. Hidden it away somewhere so that she wouldn't have to be alone. Zoë hardly ever did games.

It had worked, thought Karen, as she bent to pick up a crisp packet. Mrs Platt had banished them both to this very field. At least it was warm today. That day had been cold, misty, with a light but freezing drizzle blowing in across the football pitch. Games had been held indoors, so she and Zoë had prowled the fields alone, picking up a respectable amount of rubbish before seeking shelter in one of the semi-covered quadrangles.

Zoë had slumped onto a bench, cursing school in general and Mrs Platt in particular.

'Why don't you just do games then?' Karen had asked. 'It'd save all this hassle every week. All you'd have to do is get changed and hover round the edges. She doesn't make you do much if you're not into it.'

'All I'd 'ave to do is get changed, yeah!' Zoë mocked. ''Ave you seen the size of me lately?'

'You're not exactly fat,' Karen had tried. 'I mean, Gemma's bigger and she has a go.'

'I don't look fat in these baggy sweaters but get me in a gym kit!'

'I still don't see the problem. I mean, it's not as though anyone would say anything. Not to you. Not if they wanted to go on living, anyway.'

Zoë had laughed her special laugh. The one that meant she was getting mad.

'I think they might,' said Zoë quietly. 'If they saw. Look, can you keep a secret?'

'Sure.'

It was out before she had time to think about it. What

she should have said was no. No, I'm hopeless with secrets.

'If I tell you,' said Zoë, 'will you promise not to say anything? Not to anyone?'

Even when she'd been given this chance, Karen hadn't taken it. She had nodded meekly, with no idea of the seriousness of what she was taking on. She'd been so stupid, thought Karen, kicking a Coke can across the field. She should have known that it wasn't a spur of the moment confession. That Zoë had picked her out. Planned it all. Desperate to tell someone, Zoë had chosen her, of all people, to share her secret.

'I'm pregnant,' Zoë had announced.

It had taken a while for it to sink in. Zoë, just fifteen the previous week, pregnant. Zoë, who didn't even have a boyfriend, as far as she knew. Zoë, who had sat there, placidly smiling, as though she had announced she was going shopping or something. And among the thoughts of Zoë, other feelings had come rushing in, from a time past which she barely knew. She had spoken to push them away. To force herself to concentrate on the problem. On Zoë.

'Are you sure?' she had finally managed to mumble.

She had known the words were stupid, known even before Zoë had raised her eyebrows and started to laugh.

'Oh, yes. I'm sure.'

'Have you told your mum?'

'No. I haven't told anyone. I was going to tell Tracy when I first thought I might be, but then she's got such

35

a mouth on her, that one. It would have been all over the school before I was really sure. I've never been exactly regular...you know,' Zoë had said, looking embarrassed for the first time. 'I told myself that for ages. Pretending it wasn't true. If I'd told anyone, that would have meant it was real, see? And I didn't want it to be real. I still don't.'

'So what are you going to do?'

'Do?' Zoë had repeated vaguely.

'About the baby! Are you going to go ahead with it? Or have...'

Karen had stopped. Not able to say the words.

'An abortion?' Zoë had said. 'It's too late for that. I'm seven months.'

'Seven months!' Karen had screamed. 'Seven? Zoë, you can't be! My Auntie Pat was huge at seven months.'

'So, I'm not your flaming Auntie Pat, am I? Listen. Some women hardly have a lump at all. I read about one in the paper not long back. Didn't even know she was pregnant until the kid popped out. In the bath it was.'

'Yeah but—'

'Not everybody has a great big bulge out front. Mum didn't when she 'ad me. I've seen the photos. You couldn't tell unless you knew. She looks just like she does now. Fat.'

'You'll have to tell her, you know.'

'Says who?'

'Zoë, you'll have to. You can't keep it a secret for ever. I'm surprised she hasn't noticed! If it was my mum—'

'Well it isn't, is it? You've met my mum. Not exactly

Mastermind, is she? She wouldn't notice if I sprouted another head.'

'She'll notice a baby! And besides, you ought to see a doctor.'

'Why? I feel fine.'

'That doesn't mean the baby's fine, does it?' Karen snapped. 'You're still smoking and drinking.'

'Oh, spare me the lecture, sunshine,' Zoë had snapped. 'I'll get enough of that at home, when Mum finds out. But I can't tell her just yet.'

'Why? What's the point of putting it off?'

''Cos she'll flip, that's why. She was made up when I got moved back to top sets. Wants me to do my exams. Get a good start, as she puts it. A proper career. Not like her. She was married at eighteen, had me a year later, helped Dad build up his business and then, just when they'd got a bit of money, he buzzed off. So what's she got left? Me, that's what. How am I supposed to tell her I've messed up?'

'You're talking like it's the end of the world,' Karen had said. 'It doesn't have to be. Your mum'll help once she gets over the shock. I know she will. Bet she'll look after it while you finish at school and—'

Zoë had nudged her sharply in the ribs as a teacher walked past. They had picked up their rubbish bags and made their way slowly back to the gym.

'So you'll tell her?' Karen had urged.

'I'll have to, won't I? Eventually.'

'Soon.'

37

'Maybe. But you just remember something, eh? This is my baby. My secret. You don't tell nobody, right. Like you promised. One hint that anybody knows. One look. One snigger and you're dead, Karen. I mean it.'

Zoë had looked as though she meant it at the time. The threat had silenced Karen as much as her promise. They had talked about it since then. Many times. That was what had really drawn them together so closely. Caught Karen up. Made her an accomplice. An accomplice to what was now a criminal act. She should have known Zoë would do something crazy like this. Something desperate.

Karen shook her head, trying to force herself to think more rationally. She didn't actually know anything, of course. Only that Zoë was reaching the end of her nine months. Only that a baby had been abandoned at the medical centre, not far from Zoë's house. There was no proof to link the two together. Why had she been so quick to jump to conclusions? Why had she been so sure, the minute she'd seen the news? Because she knew Zoë, that was why. She knew just what Zoë was capable of.

The very thought made her sick. Karen doubled over, clutching her stomach, feeling the bile rise in her throat. She dropped the litter bag, spilling its contents back over the field. Not bothering to pick it all up again, she reached into her pocket and pulled out her mobile phone, looking round nervously to make sure no one was watching. You could bring your mobile into school but you weren't actually allowed to use it on the premises.

She saw the girls trooping back from the netball pitch to get changed. Waited until both they and Mrs Platt were safely back in school, then dialled Zoë's number.

It was Zoë's mum who answered, repeating her story of the previous night. Zoë was in bed. She wasn't feeling well. Flu, possibly. A bug of some sort. There was a lot of it around.

Was she serious? Was that the story Zoë had spun her? Or did she know? Was she covering up?

This time Karen was insistent to the point of rudeness. It was important. Urgent. She didn't care how sick Zoë was. She had to speak to her. Now.

It seemed an eternity before she heard Zoë's voice.

'Hi, Karen.'

Was that all she had to say?

'Er...'

Suddenly the awful accusations dried in her throat. It simply wasn't the sort of thing you could scream down the phone.

'Er, how are you? I was worried.'

'Is that it?' drawled Zoë. 'Mum said it was urgent. I thought someone had at least set fire to the school or something. No such luck, eh?'

'I mean, how do you *feel*?' Karen persisted.

'Fine.'

Fine? How could she say she felt fine?

'Apart from the bug.'

'Bug?'

'Yeah. I thought Mum told you. I've got a bug.'

39

'A bug. That's all? Nothing else?'

'No.'

'Nothing's happened?'

'No. What you on about?'

'The news. You must have seen it. You must *know*!'

'I've been in bed for three days. I haven't seen anything. Is this good news or bad news?'

'Don't play games with me, Zoë. Don't pretend!'

'Karen, 'ave you been drinking or at the glue pots or something?'

Karen stared at the phone, unable to believe what she was hearing. What was going on? Had she got it all wrong?

'I'm coming round.'

'That's nice,' said Zoë placidly. 'I could do with a bit of company. Now?'

Tempting.

'No,' said Karen, as she heard the school bell ring. 'Not now. I have to get back to school. Mrs Platt'd be sure to notice if I didn't report back. I'll come tonight. OK?'

'Fine,' said Zoë, in the instant before the phone went dead.

Karen hastily shoved some of the litter into the bag and headed back into school. She didn't get far. Mrs Platt was hovering by the side door. How much had she seen? Quite a lot, obviously. She confiscated Karen's mobile and gave her a detention for not filling the litter bag properly.

Karen did the detention that lunch time, glad to be

out of the way of all the gossip, all the snide remarks.

'My mum says it's disgusting. Dumping a kid like that!'

'Fancy just shoving it in a box. They reckon it could have been there overnight. Could have died of cold or anything!'

Under the eye of the Deputy Head the detention room was, mercifully, silent. All the offenders writing lines. Not something you needed to concentrate on. As soon as Karen's hand got into the rhythm of writing 'I must remember my games kit', she was free to think. To think back over those endless conversations with Zoë.

They usually started with: 'Have you told your mum yet?'

'I'm going to. Tonight. Honest.'

Sometimes Zoë laughed about it, making up stupid names for the baby. Ermintrude, Griselda or Dougal. At other times she cried. Every day, every conversation brought them nearer to the time and yet, even up to last week, Karen was sure that only Zoë and herself knew about it.

That was her mistake. She should have insisted, right from the beginning, that Zoë told her mother. But she hadn't. She'd allowed Zoë to manipulate her, put her off. As she'd put her off about everything else.

'What about the father?' Karen had once tentatively asked.

'What about him?'

'Who is it?'

Best to be blunt with Zoë.

'You don't need to know that. And neither does anybody else. Not ever.'

So Karen had counted back. To July, when it must have happened. Before she ever came to the school, in those blissful days when she hadn't even known of Zoë's existence.

She had made a few discreet enquiries about what had been going on then.

'Boyfriends? Zoë and Tracy?' Paula had said in response to one of her questions. 'Dunno really. They used to boast a lot. Tracy especially. Liked to make out she was dead experienced.'

'I reckon she was, too,' said Shaheen. 'Never stopped talking about what she'd been up to.'

'Tracy reckoned she was going out with a bloke who played for Leeds at one time,' Paula added. 'But nobody ever saw her with him. They never bothered with lads at school 'cept as mates. Said they liked older guys. Real men! Wouldn't lower themselves to go out with schoolboys. Not even sixth form.'

'What about the sixth formers from that Sheffield school, when we were on that geography field trip last summer?' said Shaheen. 'They made an exception for them, didn't they?'

'Oh, yeah!' Paula had said, giggling. 'Zoë and Tracy were bored out of their minds on that trip. Kept sneaking off down the pub and all sorts. There was a right fuss

42

when they were found in the lads' rooms. They almost got sent home but Mr Parsons put in a good word for them. Said they were only playing Scrabble!'

'Mr Parsons,' Karen had repeated. 'He was on that trip?'

Chapter 5

This obsession with Zoë was getting her into trouble, Karen reflected. Both at home and at school. She'd done her lunch-time detention and promptly picked up another one for daydreaming in French.

There'd be more tomorrow, if she didn't get her home-work done. But how was she supposed to concentrate? She'd rushed home from school and announced that she was going round to Zoë's.

'Oh no you're not,' her mother had said. 'Not until you've done your homework. Your dad will give you a lift, later. And pick you up. You know I don't like you hanging round that area on your own.'

Her mother was such a snob! Such a worrier. According to her mother there were psychopaths on every street corner just waiting for Karen to venture out alone after 5 p.m.!

There had been no point arguing but that hadn't stopped her trying for half an hour until her mother threatened not to let her go at all.

Karen put her books in her bag and went downstairs the minute she heard her dad coming in, mercifully early for once. If she could just get through the ordeal of dinner. But before dinner... another ordeal. The television was on. Karen could hear from halfway down the stairs.

'Police are still appealing for the mother of the baby

44

abandoned outside the medical centre to come forward.'

She wanted to turn, run back upstairs, hide away but her feet were moving all by themselves, dragging her towards the lounge, forcing her to confront the image once again.

You couldn't see the baby at the moment. Only the box. The cardboard box with WALKERS CRISPS on the outside and an abandoned child inside. Not that the baby was still inside, of course.

They were explaining that.

'The newborn baby, who nurses have called Steven, is healthy and making good progress.'

Flash to picture of baby in the arms of a nurse.

'But police fear that the mother will be traumatized and in need of medical attention and counselling. So if anybody has any information please call this number.'

The emergency number flashed on screen. Karen tried to memorize it. She would jot it down, the minute she got a chance.

Not yet. Her dad had turned round. Her mother came to announce dinner was ready. Karen was hemmed in between them, exposing her pallor, her trembling hands.

'Are you all right?'

They both spoke at once, uttering the same stupid question.

'It's awful,' was all she managed to say. 'How could she ... the mother ... ?'

She knew the answer but her parents, like everyone at school, were launching into a game of amateur psychology.

'I'm afraid,' her dad was explaining, 'it's impossible to guess until you know the full circumstances. She might be very young. Almost certainly frightened. Sick, even.'

'Sometimes,' her mother added, 'the mothers don't even know what they're doing. Sometimes, they tell themselves it's for the best. They want someone else to look after their child. Someone who can give it the love and security and—'

'Stop it!' Karen yelled. 'Stop it! Stop making excuses. They're selfish. Not sick. Not frightened. Selfish. Selfish. Selfish.'

She pushed past them and ran out of the room.

She didn't know how long she lay on her bed crying. Not long. They never left her for long. She reckoned they must have some sort of emotional egg timer down there. Give enough time for her to get whatever it was out of her system, yet not enough for her to brood.

Her parents had had plenty of practice with these sorts of scene, over the years.

The knock came first. Followed by her mother. Sitting, uninvited, on the end of the bed.

'Do you want anything to eat?'

'No. I'm not hungry.'

'Fancy coming down? I've video'd this—'

'No, thanks.'

'Karen, I know...'

'No, you don't,' said Karen quietly. 'Not this time.'

Her parents, of course, couldn't possibly be expected to know what was different about this time. They'd put it down to the fact that Karen was growing up, drifting apart from them in the normal teenage quest for independence, turning to friends for emotional support.

'I'm sorry,' said Karen. 'I don't mean to be difficult. I just can't talk about it right now.'

'That's OK,' said her mother. 'But any time you want to...'

Karen nodded.

'Is it OK if I go round to Zoë's now?'

Her dad dropped her off, as promised. Told her to phone when she was ready to come home. Karen had nodded at him, as Zoë's mum opened the door and ushered her inside.

'Go up,' she said. 'Zoë's still in bed.'

Karen stared at Zoë's mother, looking for signs. She was smiling placidly. There was no indication that she knew. No hint that upstairs was a recently pregnant daughter who had left her baby on the steps of a medical centre.

'Upstairs,' Zoë's mum repeated. 'She's upstairs.'

Zoë looked pale. Lying in bed, staring at the television. She smiled when Karen went in.

'Turn it off,' she said, pointing at the TV. 'It's boring anyway.'

Karen did as instructed and sat on the edge of the bed, waiting for Zoë to speak. 'Thanks for coming round. But you didn't have to. I feel a lot better now. I reckon I might come in to school tomorrow.'

Karen opened her mouth and closed it again. How

long was Zoë going to keep up this pretence? If it was a pretence. She tried again.

'Zoë...'

'That's my name,' said Zoë, laughing.

'Zoë, have you seen the news yet?'

'Sure. I don't usually bother but I made a point of it after you phoned. What was I supposed to be looking at?'

'The baby!' said Karen. 'The abandoned baby. The little boy. Steven.'

'Oh, that,' said Zoë. 'Yeah. Sad, isn't it? Poor little mite.'

'Sad,' said Karen, trying not to scream, not to raise her voice. 'Is that all you can say?'

'Well, it is sad. What else do you expect me to say?'

Karen stared hard at Zoë's face. Was it possible that Zoë really wasn't involved? That this wasn't Zoë's child. That Zoë was still pregnant.

'Karen,' said Zoë, 'am I missing something here? Are you tryin' to tell me something?'

Karen took a deep breath. Let out an audible sigh of relief. She'd been mistaken, that was all. She should have known. Zoë might have her faults but she wasn't that bad. Now how to explain?

'I'm sorry,' said Karen. 'I was worried, that's all. Everyone was saying it had to be a young mother. Someone who didn't want it known. Someone who was desperate. And I thought—'

'Thought what?' said Zoë. 'Go on, spit it out. I think I'm beginning to get it now.'

'I'm sorry. I know it's awful. But I thought it might be you.'

'Me?' said Zoë, eyes raised, an incredulous smile spreading over her face.

'It's not funny,' said Karen. 'I've been worried sick. Literally *sick*. What with you nearly due and living so close to the medical centre and still not having told your mother as far as I know. It was possible!'

'No,' said Zoë, 'I'm still not quite with you. What was nearly due?'

'Zoë, don't pretend to be stupid,' Karen snapped. 'This is hard enough as it is.'

She dropped her voice before adding, 'I was right about one thing. You still haven't told her, have you? You haven't told your mum you're pregnant?'

'I haven't told her for a very good reason.'

'Yeah, I know. She'll be disappointed. She wants you to do your exams.'

'No,' said Zoë. 'Not that.'

'What then?' said Karen. 'What's the good reason now?'

'I haven't told my mum I'm pregnant,' said Zoë slowly, 'for the very good reason that I'm not. Never was.'

Karen had expected all manner of excuses. A whole range of possibilities had flooded into her mind. But this? Total and flat denial.

'But ... but ...'

'Get a grip, Karen,' laughed Zoë. 'You sound like stuttering Stella when the teacher asks her a question.'

'But,' said Karen, finally wrapping her mind round

what she wanted to say, 'you told me. You know you did. All those conversations! It's all we've talked about for over two months.'

'Yeah, well, you've got to talk about something, 'aven't you?' said Zoë, laughing again. 'I mean, after Tracy left, I thought I was just going to die of boredom hangin' around with you three. I mean, no offence, but discussions about maths homework and the latest Terry Pratchett novel don't exactly grab me. So I thought I'd liven things up a bit. Invent a little secret for you and me to get our teeth into. No point trying to tell Paula and Shaheen. They know me too well. They'd have seen through it from the word go.'

'Now wait a minute,' said Karen. 'Let me get this straight. Are you telling me you made it up? The whole thing? Just for fun?'

Zoë nodded. 'Look, I'm sorry. I mean, how was I supposed to know you'd take it so seriously? I didn't really expect you to believe me at all. You don't know me as well as the others but you surely must have clocked what a liar I am! I mean, you said yourself, I never even looked pregnant. See,' she added, swinging her legs out of bed and standing up for inspection. 'Fat, that's all. Bulges everywhere but no lumps up front. No babies.'

She patted her stomach as she spoke, before crawling back into bed.

'All that proves,' said Karen, 'is that you're not pregnant now. But you were, weren't you? I was right, wasn't I? That baby, Steven—'

'Oh heck,' said Zoë, looking genuinely distressed. 'I

50

wish I'd never started this. And I'm sorry, OK? I mean how was I supposed to know that some nutter would abandon a kid and you'd be daft enough to think it was mine?'

'So if you weren't pregnant, weren't ever pregnant,' said Karen, 'how come you carried on your little joke for so long? How come you didn't tell me earlier?'

'You got so involved in it all,' said Zoë. 'I didn't like to disappoint you. Besides I thought it'd be fun to see how long you'd go on believing. You were just so incredibly gullible. I mean, can't you count? I was already past the imaginary nine months, you know. Would you still have been waiting after ten or eleven?'

'Don't,' said Karen. 'Stop it. I don't know what you think you're playing at but—'

'Playing,' said Zoë. 'Now you're getting it. Just a bit of fun. Ask anybody at school. Ask Shaheen and Paula. Me and Tracy used to have people on all the time. Haven't they told you about how Tracy was goin' out with that Leeds player? We strung people along with that for ages. Tracy's real boyfriend at the time was a car mechanic who played for some third-rate Sunday team! Then there was that time I bunked off school for two months, no questions asked, just 'cos I said my mum had cancer.'

'That's disgusting!' Karen screamed. 'Sick! Perverted!'

'Well, I was only eleven then,' said Zoë, as if that explained everything. 'I wouldn't make up anything that bad now.'

'You just have, according to you,' said Karen.

51

'Oh stop making such a big deal of it, will you?' Zoë snapped. 'It was harmless enough. It wouldn't have come to nothing if it hadn't been for this complication. This Steven kid. I feel sorry about that, I really do. But he's not mine, OK?'

Chapter 6

'How do I know that?' said Karen, almost to herself. 'How am I supposed to know what's true any more?'

'Come on,' said Zoë reassuringly. 'Think about it. Think what you're saying. According to you I get through a full pregnancy without anybody, not even my mum, suspecting. I have the baby. Where, Karen? Here? Out in a field? In the middle of the city centre, or what? Let's say here. I have a baby and my mum never even notices. I know I said she was thick but she's here all the time and I should think even she knows the difference between childbirth and a bout of flu. So, then I take this baby, which Mum hasn't noticed, to the medical centre, nip back, have breakfast and pretend nothing's happened?'

'Well somebody did,' Karen muttered.

'Somebody who lives on their own,' Zoë said. 'Not someone who lives with their flaming mother, for heaven's sake! And almost certainly...'

Karen waited for Zoë to add her bit of amateur psychology to everyone else's. 'And almost certainly someone who was pregnant in the first place. Unlike me!'

'I don't believe this,' said Karen, her eyes filling up with tears. 'I don't believe you've done this. Have you any idea how I've felt these last two months? What I've been through these last few days? And for what? A joke!'

She leapt up and kicked the side of the bed.

'No need to throw a wobbler on me,' said Zoë. 'I've said I'm sorry, 'aven't I? Me and Tracy used to pull silly tricks on each other all the time. I mean, I actually got the idea from her! She tried to con me more than once that she was pregnant! She never was. It was always a laugh. A bit of fun.'

'Fun,' Karen repeated. 'Phantom pregnancies were your and Tracy's idea of fun?'

'Sure. Why not? I mean, if you don't have a sense of humour, that's your problem really. How was I supposed to know you were so naive and sensitive?'

'Sensitive!' Karen screamed at her. 'Oh yeah, I'm sensitive all right.'

It was on the tip of her tongue. She was right on the verge of telling Zoë why she was like she was. Why the sight of abandoned Christmas puppies, let alone babies, made her cry. Why she shredded those charity leaflets which featured pictures of wide-eyed, orphaned children. Why she hated deception, irresponsibility, lies. Why these things made her burn with an anger she could barely control. The anger was burning now, devouring all sense, all rationality. If she stayed a minute longer it would all come out.

Karen didn't even pause to say goodbye to either Zoë or her mother. She stumbled downstairs, pushed open the door and ran out into the street. Kept on running until breath deserted her.

She paused, leaning against a wall, feeling for the first time the heavy rain dripping down her face and into her eyes. She looked at her watch. Ten past nine. She shouldn't have run out like that. She should have phoned her dad as instructed. Asked him to pick her up. Too late now. There was no way she was going back to Zoë's and she'd forgotten to pick up her mobile from Mrs Platt at the end of school.

She looked up and down the street she had found herself in. No sign of a phone box but there was a bus stop further down. She could get a bus into the city centre and from there home was just another bus ride, or taxi ride, or phone call away.

The street was deserted, the bus shelter full of litter and graffiti but mercifully dry. She pulled a comb and mirror from her bag. The mirror was fairly useless, it was so dark, but pulling the comb through her thick hair made her feel slightly better. A bit more human, as it were. A car slowed down, as she was putting her comb away. She shivered. Perhaps her mum was right about the nutters who lurked on street corners. You read about such a lot of cases these days.

She pressed up close to the side of the bus shelter, fears for her safety subsiding as the car passed on, allowing her thoughts to return to that other story she'd been reading a lot about. Baby Steven.

Zoë's baby? Probably not. A doctor would be able to tell but Zoë wasn't likely to see one. And Karen could hardly tell anyone now.

'Er, I think my friend might be the mother of that baby.'

There'd be a right stink if she was wrong. Zoë might even sue or something. And besides, Zoë's new story made more sense than the old one. She never had been pregnant. It was all a pack of lies. Lies. Lies.

And if not Zoë's baby, then whose? Almost certainly someone local. Probably someone young. Maybe people at school hadn't been so wide of the mark with Tracy. What if one of Tracy's pregnancies had turned out to be more than a joke? But, in a sense, it didn't really matter to Karen who the mother was. What worried her, what tore at her every nerve, was thinking about the child.

Karen suddenly jumped as she felt a hand brush against her shoulder. She'd been so lost in her depressing thoughts, she hadn't noticed the footsteps. Hadn't known that someone had crept up behind her.

'Watch it!' said a voice as Karen swung round, ready to scream. 'You trod on my foot then. I've got mud all over my new shoes, look.'

The figure, bending down, wiping the shoes with delicate fingertips, was easy to identify, even though the blonde hair was a shorter than it had previously been.

'I thought it was you,' said Tracy as she stood upright again. 'What you doin' round here then?'

'I could ask you the same question,' said Karen, trying to avoid any mention of Zoë.

'I live just there,' said Tracy, indicating a row of houses. 'At least for the moment. We're moving soon. To a detached. Once my modelling money comes through.'

Karen tried a faint smile. Truth or fiction? Who cared? Such matters were minor league now.

'What are you looking at?' said Tracy.

Karen realized that she'd been staring. Looking for signs of guilt or trauma on Tracy's immaculately made-up face. Or signs that the twig-thin figure had recently sported a bulge. Getting drawn in by stupid rumours. Why should Tracy be any more of a suspect than any other female in this part of the city? Just because she had a bit of a reputation.

'Er, nothing,' said Karen. 'You look nice.'

'Oh, right,' said Tracy. 'You going into town, then?'

'I'm going home. It's easier to go into the city centre first.'

As she spoke, the bus appeared. Karen sort of hoped that Tracy would go off and sit on her own. They had hardly been big mates. But no such luck.

'What've you been doing then?' said Tracy, eyeing her in the brighter light of the bus. 'You look like a manically depressed, half-drowned rat.'

'Thanks,' said Karen.

'Well you do,' said Tracy. 'And your eyes are all puffy. You've been crying, haven't you?'

'Er, yes. We, er, had to have our cat put to sleep.'

It was catching, this lying business. They didn't even have a cat but Tracy wasn't to know that.

'Oh, no,' she said, with genuine sympathy. 'I know how you feel. I cried for ages when our Felix got run over.'

Karen looked down at her feet, guilty for having dredged up memories of the departed Felix, as Tracy related the whole sorry story. Funny, you never thought of girls like Tracy having pets, let alone loving them.

'Tell me about your modelling,' said Karen, as soon as Tracy stopped talking about poor Felix.

Karen wasn't really interested but was keen to while away the rest of the journey with something harmless.

'It's going great,' said Tracy. 'Loads of magazine work coming in. My agent says I've got the right look for this millennium. Best thing I ever did, quitting school. How is the old dump, by the way? How's Zoë?'

'Fine,' said Karen, trying not to betray anything with her eyes.

'Only I've been thinking about her recently,' said Tracy. 'I saw something in the paper. Zoë, I thought! That has to be Zoë! Hang on, this is my stop.'

'Me too,' said Karen, standing up, desperate to hear whether Tracy's thoughts were the same as her own.

'No, you want to go on to the bus station, don't you?'

'Er, no. I think I'll just find a phone box. Call my dad.'

'Phone box?' said Tracy, as though she barely knew what one was. 'Where's your mobile?'

'In school, with Mrs Platt,' said Karen.

'Not to worry,' said Tracy, as they got off the bus. 'You can use mine.'

'Er, thanks,' said Karen.

But she knew she couldn't make the call until she heard the end of Tracy's sentence. How on earth had

Tracy connected Zoë with the newspaper story? Tracy wasn't supposed to know anything.

'Tell you what,' said Tracy, nodding in the direction of a pub. 'I'm meeting my boyfriend in there. He's always late. Nip in with me and you can have a quick drink while you wait for your dad.'

Karen wasn't sure how she was going to explain to her dad why she was phoning from one of the seediest pubs in the city but she would cross that bridge when she had to.

Once settled at a small table in the corner of the dimly lit bar, Tracy handed over her mobile and went off to buy drinks.

'He's on his way,' said Karen, when Tracy returned. 'Now what were you saying about Zoë?'

Not subtle, but time was running out. It wouldn't take her dad long to get there. Fifteen minutes at the most.

'I was asking how she was.'

'Not that. Afterwards. You said you'd been thinking about her. Something you saw in the paper.'

'Oh that,' said Tracy. 'I had to go to London to this agency and on the train I was reading a paper that someone had left lying around. It had this new diet in it. I thought it would suit Zoë 'cos it had loads of fruit in it. She likes fruit.'

'Fruit?' Karen repeated.

'Yeah, you know. Apples, oranges, pears...'

'The article you saw was about a diet?' said Karen, knowing how dim she sounded.

'Yeah! You look disappointed. Were you expecting something else?'

'Er, no. Not really. It was just something Zoë told me recently. I thought you might know. I mean, you know her better than anyone. Does she make stuff up?'

'Like what?'

'Lies. Stories about herself.'

'Doesn't everybody? I lie about my age all the time. My boyfriend thinks I'm twenty.'

'I meant more serious stuff. Would you say she was a compulsive liar or anything?'

'Definitely,' said Tracy, nodding knowledgeably. 'And she's good. Caught me out a few times. Most of the time it was only in fun. We were both as bad! But Zoë... Well, yeah, Zoë can take it a bit far sometimes. I mean it's 'cos of her stories I ended up quitting school. That business with Mr Parsons was all her fault.'

'But I thought—'

'So did everyone else! Tracy. Villain of the piece. Leading poor little Zoë astray as usual. D'you want to know what really happened?'

Karen nodded. Truth or lies, she would listen. Try to piece together any insights into Zoë's character. Try to work out what made her tick.

'It won't matter now,' said Tracy, 'with me left and him gone, but I'd rather you didn't say anything to Zoë. She was dead keen for me to keep it quiet.'

Karen nodded again. More secrets.

'That day, when we were drinking, the silly cow told

me she was pregnant.'

'She told you that!' said Karen, remembering that Zoë had denied telling Tracy anything. 'Wasn't she scared you'd let on?'

'Not me,' said Tracy. 'I don't blab. I've never told anybody about this before, for a start! It's Zoë who's got a mouth on her. You can't tell her nothing. Anyway, like I say, we'd had a lot to drink and I didn't take it too seriously. We were always having each other on about stupid things. But she wouldn't let it drop. Kept going on about it. Said it happened when we went away with the school.'

'Did you believe her?'

'Did I heck! She wouldn't be that stupid for a start. She knows more about contraception than the school nurse who gives all the talks. Zoë just makes things up for a bit of a laugh or attention or something. Anyway, you know what it's like when you're drunk?'

Karen nodded, though in fact she had no idea.

'I sort of kept the joke going. Teased her about who the father was. Mr Parsons was on that trip. We got a bit giggly and I said I was going to ask him about it. I wasn't, of course. I was just mucking. I headed for his room, intending to walk past and on to registration. But Zoë was egging me on.

'"Go on then," she said. "Ask him. I dare you. Ask him what really happened on that trip."

'In the end,' said Tracy, 'she confronted him.'

'Zoë did?' Karen asked.

Tracy nodded before going on to explain.

'"Sir," Zoë said, "remember that school trip we went on? Remember what happened? Well, I'm pregnant."'

'She told Mr Parsons she was pregnant?' said Karen, trying to come to terms with this latest twist.

'Yep! Up till then,' said Tracy, 'I hadn't believed a word. I thought it was one of her stories. But he went white. Absolutely white. I've never seen anyone go like that before. So then I put two and two together and started screaming at him. I'd had half a bottle of vodka, remember. I think I went for him and he tried to hold me back.'

'So why didn't any of this come out? Why all the lies? The cover-ups?'

'Zoë begged me not to say anything. Told me to crack on he'd made a pass at me. She asked me to keep it quiet till she'd decided what to do.'

'And what about him?'

'Well, he wasn't going to say anything, was he? I've never seen anyone look so scared. I reckon he was glad to go with so little hassle.'

'So, you're saying Zoë's story was true,' said Karen slowly. 'You're saying she was pregnant?'

'I'm saying she thought she was. Genuinely thought so. I'm saying he looked as if he knew something about it. That's all. Why? What does it matter?'

'What does it matter?' said Karen incredulously. 'A man lost his job for a start. And then, there's Zoë. Haven't you been in touch? Didn't you ever wonder what happened to the baby?'

'Oh, I know what happened,' said Tracy casually.

'Do you?'

'Yeah. Zoë phoned me after I quit school. Told me to stop worrying. It was a false alarm. She thought she was but she wasn't. These scares happen. I should know!'

'It was only a scare? That's what she told you?'

'Yes.'

'And you believed her?'

'As much as I ever believe anything she says. But it must have been something like that. I mean, that was months ago and she's not pregnant now, is she?'

'No,' said Karen thoughtfully. 'She's certainly not pregnant now.'

Chapter 7

'I feel sick,' Karen groaned on Wednesday morning, as she pushed the cereal bowl towards her mother.

'Were you drinking last night?'

'No. I told you. Tracy was round at Zoë's and I said I'd get the bus with her for a bit of company. I had a Coke, that's all.'

More lies. Tracy hadn't been at Zoë's and she'd bought Karen lager, not Coke. But she'd only had a few sips. Hardly enough to make you feel sick the next day!

'So why do you feel sick?'

'How should I know?' Karen snapped. 'Bug or something.'

She could hardly say it was the radio that had made her feel sick. Baby Steven was still the lead item on the local news. The mother still hadn't come forward. Police were still concerned for her safety.

If only she'd turn up, whoever she was, that would solve the problem. At least part of it. It would prove that Zoë's only crime was to tell a stupid, callous pack of lies. And if the mother didn't turn up? What then? What would that prove? Tracy's evidence had seemed to point the finger firmly back in Zoë's direction, but how could you be sure?

'Shall I phone the school?'

'What?' said Karen.

'Phone and tell them you're sick.'

'No. I'll go. I'll be fine. Honest.'

Lies again. She had no intention of going to school. And she wouldn't be fine. Not ever. Not until she knew.

It was a crazy idea, Karen thought, as the bus jolted along towards the hospital. But, for the moment, it was the only idea she had. If she could see baby Steven, just for a minute, maybe it would help. The glimpses she'd caught on television didn't help at all. All babies looked more or less the same, especially at a distance from behind a camera. But if she could see him for real, maybe it would tell her something.

Or was she fooling herself? Karen thought, as she approached the main doors of the hospital. Did she have other, private reasons for wanting to see him? Best not to examine her motives too deeply. Best just to do it.

Not such an easy matter. Karen knew nothing about hospitals or their security systems. Her family were blessed with excellent health. All four grandparents were alive and thriving. Her parents had, mercifully, never suffered anything worse than a nasty cold and, consequently, Karen couldn't remember ever having set foot in a hospital before. Not since she was a baby. And, of course, she didn't remember that – only knew because of the photographs she kept in the drawer under her bed.

The main doors slid open automatically as she approached. No problem there. She studied the large board on which the various floors and wards were listed.

Where would he be? Children's ward? No. Baby unit. Maternity. Surely?

She took the lift and followed the signs along the corridor. Nobody tried to stop her. Nobody asked what she was doing. And why should they? There were patients and visitors all over the place. She could be checking in for an appointment. Visiting a sick aunt.

Getting into the ward would be a little trickier. She hovered on the corridor, watching for a while, until she got the hang of the system. There was an intercom, which you had to speak into before the door would open. No point even trying that. What would she say?

'Hi, I'm Karen. I've come to see if I can guess whether my friend is the mother of baby Steven!'

Some chance. But joy of great joys! Karen stared, unable to believe her luck. A nurse or assistant of some sort was pushing an enormous laundry basket on wheels through the doorway. She left it, propping the door open, as she turned back to pick up some bits that had fallen off the top.

Karen moved more quickly than she had thought possible, squeezing in along the side of the basket, pushing open a door on the right, and stepping inside, as the woman returned. Karen was in a cupboard. Shelves piled high with sheets, towels and nappies. But, no matter. She was on the ward. If it was the right one...

Pressing her ear to the door, she listened. She couldn't hear anything. Carefully, she eased open the door and crept out. Facing her, at the top of the short corridor, was a reception desk. A nurse was occupied on the telephone, holding the receiver with one hand and tapping a keyboard with the other. She seemed to be looking for information, her eyes fixed on the screen.

Karen decided on the bold approach. She strode forward, walking confidently past reception, turning the corner and stopping to consider her next move. It was as far as she got.

'Excuse me,' a voice behind her said.

Karen turned and faced the nurse from reception.

'Can I help you?'

An innocent enough question but the nurse looked puzzled, sceptical. And why shouldn't she be, confronted by a girl in school uniform prowling round the baby unit, unannounced, on a Wednesday morning? Karen cursed herself for acting so hastily. She should have thought it out, made up some plausible reason for being here.

'Er, yes,' she said, thinking quickly as she spoke. 'I'm Karen. I phoned earlier in the week. About a project I'm doing at school. Baby care. The lady I spoke to said I could come and look round.'

Not bad, for the spur of the moment, Karen thought. She doubted whether Zoë herself could have done better.

'Oh,' said the nurse. 'No one mentioned it. It's not in the diary. Who did you speak to?'

'Er, Sister, er, I've forgotten the name. I've got it written down, somewhere.'

She pretended to fish around in her pockets.

'Sorry, can't seem to find it. I'm sure I had it.'

'Not to worry,' said the nurse. 'I'll get someone to help.'

So far, so good. Karen waited until the nurse was out of sight before moving on, looking into the side wards as she went. Babies with mothers. Mothers with babies. No sign of babies on their own, of baby Steven. Twin babies with mum. Baby with mum and dad. Baby with nurse. Nurse, not mum. There was no mother in this room. Maybe she'd popped to the loo or maybe this was Steven.

'Karen?'

She turned as she heard the strange voice speak her name. The strange voice which belonged to a lady with the word 'Sister' on her uniform.

'There seems to have been some mix-up, love,' the lady continued. 'Are you sure you've got the right hospital?'

'I don't know,' said Karen. 'I think so. I'm sure it was . . .'

Suddenly, everything changed. Everything went wrong. All the words she was trying to say stuck in her throat and something entirely different came out.

'Is that Steven?' she said, pointing at the glass partition. 'Is that the baby I heard about on the news?'

'No,' said Sister. 'That's a little girl. Why?'

'I just wondered,' said Karen. 'He is here though? In this hospital?'

The Sister nodded, looking at her as quizzically as the receptionist had done. Too late to backtrack now. May as well press on.

'Only I was interested,' said Karen, 'with me doing this project on babies and then seeing him on the news. I thought I might cut out some articles. Do a bit about him.'

She knew it sounded lame. Pathetic. But Sister seemed taken in.

'That sounds like a good idea.'

'I couldn't – I mean, it's probably not allowed – but I couldn't . . . could I see him?'

There. It was done. Out. Sister could only say no.

'I think that could be arranged, if you really wanted to. We have to be very careful, you understand. Security reasons. Especially with cases like Steven. But I could take you, if you like.'

Karen nodded. This was unbelievably easy. Better than she could possibly have hoped for.

'If you'll just excuse me,' Sister said. 'I've got something to sort out first. I'll only be a minute.'

Less than a minute, Karen thought. She barely had time to adjust her thoughts before Sister returned, as if she'd been scared to leave Karen alone. Not surprising. You didn't want strangers lurking on baby wards. Even fairly harmless-looking schoolgirls. People took babies sometimes. Karen had read of a case recently and had thought it was somehow unfair that some people were desperate enough to steal a child while others casually abandoned or abused them.

They walked to a room at the very end of the ward. Walked very slowly. Sister talked all the time, as though she wanted deliberately to impede their progress.

'Is this project part of your exam courses then?'

'No, it's something extra. Free choice. For P.S.E. Personal and Social Education,' she explained, in case

Sister wasn't familiar with modern schools.

'And which school do you go to?'

'Just the local comp,' said Karen, anxious not to give too much away.

'You live round here, do you?'

'Not far.'

'And do your parents know you've come on this, er, visit today?'

'I think they had to sign a form ages ago,' Karen muttered.

'Here we are then.'

Sister pushed open a door. There were two ladies in the room already. Both young. One in a nurse's uniform, the other in a suit. The Sister nodded at the nurse, who immediately left.

'Miss Hobbs,' said Sister, introducing the other lady. 'She's the key social worker assigned to Steven. And this is Karen. She's asked to see Steven as part of a project she's doing at school.'

There was something in Sister's voice, as she spoke. Something about the social worker's grip as they shook hands. Something that sounded like – felt like – sympathy, pity almost.

Karen didn't have time to analyse too deeply. Her eyes had already made contact with the sleeping baby. Only a few days old, he already had wisps of dark hair. Dark, like Zoë. No, she told herself. Dark like herself. Like half the population! There was nothing in the screwed-up, tiny, sleeping face that suggested Zoë any more than it suggested anyone else. What had she expected? A sign stamped on his forehead? *My mother is . . . ?*

Sleeping, in blissful ignorance, he wouldn't even know. Know that he was any different from any other baby here. When did that sort of consciousness start? When would he realize? When would he be told? When would he start to understand? To search inside himself for what would always be missing.

She felt the arm around her shoulder, almost before she realized she had started to cry. Not even quiet tears but sharp, hysterical sobs, tearing through her shaking body. Sister was leading her out. Back down the corridor.

'I'm sorry,' Karen managed to mutter.

'It's all right, love. It'll be all right. I'm glad you came. You did the right thing.'

Glad? Right thing? What was she on about? Before Karen could pull herself together to question further, she was steered into an office, eased into a chair. Sister and Miss Hobbs were standing by. And near the window, someone else. Someone in uniform. Not a nurse's uniform. A policewoman's uniform. Karen tried to stand but immediately Sister was kneeling beside her, placing a restraining hand on her arm.

'It's all right,' Sister said. 'No one's going to harm you. We just need to talk to you. That's all.'

'Why?' said Karen, cursing herself for having given her real name, for turning up in a uniform which would hardly be difficult to trace to her school. 'I haven't done anything wrong!'

'Not wrong, love, no,' said the Sister. 'But there isn't a school project, is there?'

How did they know? They could only be guessing.

'Not exactly. It was something extra I decided to do.'

She had to bluff it out. There was no other way. To tell the truth would mean revealing her fears about Zoë. And she couldn't do that. Not with nothing more than a hunch and Zoë's tangle of lies to go on.

'What have I done?' said Karen, as she felt three pairs of eyes resting on her. 'Why are the police here? I wasn't going to harm him. I just wanted to see him.'

'Of course you did,' said Sister.

Of course. Why did she say of course? What could she possibly know about it? What on earth was she thinking?

Suddenly Karen knew what Sister was thinking. What they were all thinking. What anyone would think if a teenager turned up demanding to look at an abandoned baby, bursting into tears the minute she saw it. How could she have been so stupid? So utterly, utterly stupid.

'No,' she screamed out. 'No. You've got it all wrong. I'm not the mother. That's what you think, isn't it? Well, I'm not. I'm not.'

Chapter 8

The wait seemed endless, sitting in that tiny office, waiting for her parents to turn up. Determined to stay silent. Refusing to say anything that might incriminate her. Or, more importantly, incriminate Zoë. Fearing that she would say something stupid the moment she opened her mouth.

She knew she was safe enough. As soon as her parents arrived, the basic misunderstanding would be cleared up. Her parents would explain how and why it couldn't possibly be her. They could explain other things too, if they had to. Information given in whispered confidentiality.

Maybe she should volunteer the information herself? But no. It was too painful, too impossible to talk about. With luck, it wouldn't need to come out at all.

At worst, her parents would have to tell the nurse, the social worker and the policewoman why Karen did strange things sometimes. They would understand. It was in their nature, their work, to understand. Her secret, her own, personal secret, would be safe with them.

It would serve, too, as an explanation to her parents. They would not question why she chose to go prowling round a hospital in search of a strange baby. They would think they knew the answer and she would not enlighten them further. There would be no need to mention Zoë.

Her mother arrived first, followed about ten minutes later by her dad. It was as Karen had expected. Embarrassment on all sides, but within the hour, she was free to leave.

'I'm sorry,' Sister muttered, not for the first time, as she showed them out. 'But, naturally, I was concerned. I mean, we're expecting the mother to be very young.'

'It's all right,' said Karen's mother tactfully. 'An understandable mistake. And we're sorry Karen caused so much trouble but—'

'I understand,' said Sister.

Karen chose to go back to school. Better than hanging around at home, listening to her mother trying to be helpful. Dad wrote a note, explaining how Karen was a bit late as she'd been to hospital. A lie, yet not a lie. Sometimes you had to bend the truth a bit. But how did it become a habit? A lifestyle almost, in Zoë's case?

Zoë. Another whole day thinking about Zoë, becoming more determined as the day wore on, to get to the truth. But how? By the time the final bell went, Karen had decided on one more try, one last effort to appeal to Zoë's better nature, if she had one.

Karen rescued her mobile from Mrs Platt, stood outside the school gates and phoned her mother with the lie that she was staying on at school for an extra orchestra rehearsal and then headed off to Zoë's.

'You're getting to be quite a regular visitor,' Zoë's mum said. 'I'm glad. Zoë doesn't see much of anyone any more. Not since Tracy got too high and mighty for the likes of

74

us. Go up. She's still in bed. Can't seem to shake this bug off at all. She's got no energy.'

Zoë put down her magazine as Karen entered the room and sat down on the edge of the bed.

'Didn't think I'd see you again,' said Zoë. 'I was going to make the effort to come into school this mornin' only I thought you'd still be mad at me and there didn't seem any point.'

'I wasn't in school,' said Karen.

'You haven't been bunkin' off, have you?' said Zoë, looking at her uniform. 'Not our Karen!'

'I went to the hospital.'

'Why? You not well or something?'

'*The* hospital. The maternity ward. I went to see the baby.'

'What d'you do that for? You loony!' Zoë snapped.

'I just wanted to see him.'

'And did you?'

'Yes.'

'And they let you? Just like that? You didn't tell them anything? You didn't say you thought he was mine!'

'No,' said Karen. 'No, I didn't. Not even when they got the police in.'

'The police. Why? They didn't think you were tryin' to abduct him?'

'They thought I was the mother.'

Zoë stared at her and nodded. 'Yeah,' she said. 'Yeah. I suppose they would. How the heck did you get out of that one?'

'They got my parents in. They just explained how it couldn't possibly have been me. I mean, like you said, how could anyone have a baby without their parents knowing?'

'But didn't anyone wonder why you were so interested?'

'Not really,' said Karen hastily. 'I mean, loads of people are fascinated by the case. I just made out I was curious. They probably thought I was a bit of a nutter.'

'You are,' said Zoë. 'Honestly, Karen, this has got to stop before you get us both into trouble. You sure you didn't say anything?'

'Why?' said Karen. 'What if I had said something? What are you so scared about? The very worst that could happen is that they'd get you to see a doctor. Then they'd know, wouldn't they? We'd all know.'

'I know now, thank you very much,' said Zoë. 'And so would you if you weren't so thick.'

'I saw Tracy the other night,' said Karen, ignoring the insult.

'That's nice,' said Zoë calmly. 'How is she?'

'Fine,' said Karen. 'Modelling's going great, so she says, anyway.'

'All right for some.'

'She told me something,' Karen blurted out. 'She told me about that business with Mr Parsons. About what really happened.'

'Sure,' said Zoë, propping herself up on the pillows. 'Which version is this?'

'The version where you told her you were pregnant.'

'Did I? Don't remember pulling that trick on her. I seem to remember it was the other way round.'

'Do you remember telling Mr Parsons you were pregnant?'

'Nope.'

'Are you going to go on denying all this for ever?'

'For the last time, I'm not denying anything. And if that's all you're going to bleat on about, you'd better go. I'm getting right cheesed off with it.'

'OK,' said Karen. 'I'm going.'

As she stood up to leave, the bedroom door opened.

'Your mum's been on the phone, Karen,' Zoë's mother said. 'Wanted to know if you were here. She was in a right flap because she's not getting an answer from your mobile.'

'She wouldn't,' said Karen. 'I've got it switched off.'

'Anyway, she wants you to go home straight away.'

'I'm on my way,' said Karen, as Zoë's mum waddled off downstairs.

Karen paused at the door and looked back at Zoë. One more try. One more appeal.

'Don't you want to know how he was?' she asked.

'Who?'

'The baby!'

'I suppose you want to tell me?'

'He was gorgeous, Zoë. Really small. At least he looked small but the social worker said he was a good weight and feeding well.'

'Social worker? What's he need one of them for? He's not a delinquent already, is he?'

'He needs a social worker to find him a family,' Karen snapped, irritated by Zoë's flippant attitude.

'You mean if his mother doesn't turn up?'

'Obviously.'

'And if she did,' said Zoë slowly, 'what do you suppose would happen then?'

'I don't know,' said Karen. 'I suppose it would depend on her circumstances, her health, whatever. I suppose she could still decide to put the baby up for adoption.'

'They'd let her do that?'

'I expect so. If that was what she wanted,' said Karen.

'So why bother coming forward? If the result's going be the same anyway? Why not save yourself the trouble.'

Karen turned back from the door where she had been hovering and sat on the end of the bed.

'Yourself.'

'What?' said Zoë.

'You said, save yourself the trouble. Not herself. Shouldn't it have been herself?'

'That's better,' said Zoë, laughing. 'Change the subject. Let's talk about the finer points of English grammar. It was a figure of speech, that's all.'

As Karen mulled over the possibility, there was a knock at the door.

'Sorry, girls,' said Zoë's mum. 'Didn't want to intrude but your mum's been on again, Karen. Asking if you'd left yet and whether you'd like her to come and pick you up. She wants to speak to you.'

'Can you just tell her I'm on my way?' said Karen, irritated by the interruption, just as she was making some progress.

'I'll try but she's in a bit of a state. Is she always like this? She sounded dead uptight. Said you'd been acting a bit strange, lately. I mean, I told her! That's teenage girls for you, I said. I never know the time of day with Zoë, these days. Talk about mood swings! Getting up and going for walks in the middle of the night—'

'All right, Mum,' said Zoë. 'Karen gets the picture.'

'I'm beginning to,' said Karen.

'Anyway,' said Zoë's mum, 'I'd better go and talk to her again. Do I say you're on your way or you want a lift or what?'

Karen opened her mouth to speak but it was Zoë's voice she heard.

'Tell her Karen's fine. There's no problem. Tell her Karen's staying for tea.'

'I don't know whether she'll be happy with that,' said Zoë's mum.

'I don't care whether she's happy or not! Talk to her. Sort it out, can't you?' Zoë snapped.

'I'll have a go,' said her mum placidly. 'Tea's nothing special, I'm afraid, Karen. Fish fingers and chips. Will that do you?'

'Sounds nice,' said Karen, 'but I can't stay.'

'She can,' said Zoë, scrambling out of bed and more

79

or less pushing her mother out.

Zoë positioned herself by the door as Karen tried to follow.

'Don't be ridiculous,' said Karen. 'You can't make me stay. You can't make me keep quiet either. I've already decided. I'm going to tell my mum. Tell her what you told me. Tell her what I think. She'll know what to do.'

'You don't have to do that, Karen. At least not now. Not yet. Sit down. Come on. Please. Don't dump on me, Karen. I'll tell you. I'll tell you everything that happened. And then you've got to help me.'

Against all her instincts, Karen allowed Zoë to steer her back, sitting with her on the end of the bed. 'You were right,' whispered Zoë. 'You were right all along. The baby's mine.'

Chapter 9

'Why?' said Karen, her voice echoing Zoë's whisper. 'Why did you do it? How could you?'

'Are we talking technically or emotionally here?'

'Zoë!' said Karen, trying to keep her voice low and controlled. 'I don't believe you! You're not even serious about it.'

'Oh, I'm serious all right.'

'So?'

'So it was easy. In a way. No, don't butt in,' she said, as Karen opened her mouth. 'Let me try an' explain it. In my own way. I'd known I was pregnant for ages, right? But when it happened, it was as though it was a big surprise. I still hadn't got around to telling anyone. 'Cept you. And Tracy. But then I fobbed Tracy off by saying it was a false alarm and, as far as I know, she never thought no more about it. We don't see each other any more, so why should she? I kept meaning to tell Mum but I just never got round to it. And then it happened. Saturday night, I didn't feel too good. Stomach cramps. I know this sounds crazy, under the circumstances, but I sort of convinced myself it was a bug.'

Zoë shrugged her shoulders and smiled.

'Sunday it was worse. I couldn't get out of bed. Then it sort of gradually dawned on me. Blimey, I thought, I'm going into labour! And all I could think was, how the heck am I going to explain this to Mum? I was going over speeches in my head. I'd just got it all worked out, how to put it to her, tactful like, when at about three o'clock in the afternoon, he turned up.'

'Who?' said Karen, as Zoë seemed to have come to a complete stop.

'My dad. He was on his own. He doesn't bring his new partner here. Wouldn't dare! Mum'd kill her, I reckon. Anyway, he came up to see me. All gushing and friendly, until I reminded him about missing my birthday and how he was two months behind with his payments.

Anyway, he sort of looked a bit embarrassed and said that was what he'd come about. I expected him to slip me fifty quid at least, but oh, no. He shouted to my mum to come up and started on this bleeding hearts story. About recession and how his business had never quite picked up. Well, to cut a long story short, he said we hadn't a chance of getting any more money out of him for a bit.'

Karen tried to look sympathetic, wondering where this story was getting them.

'There was a right row,' Zoë went on. 'My mum pointed out that he'd managed three foreign holidays, lately, that she knew about. I mean, when he was with us, we'd be lucky to get a day trip to Filey, let alone a month in Egypt and wherever else he's been. And he said that was before he realized how bad things had got. And, of course, me and Mum didn't believe a word, 'cos he's a right liar.'

The word brought Karen to her senses. For a moment

there, she'd started to feel genuine sympathy for Zoë, but then how could you guarantee how much of this was true?

'D'you know,' said Zoë, 'he'd been carrying on his affair for two years before Mum even found out? Two years of weekend conferences and meetings that never existed. And all the time he had the cheek to be lecturing me about commitments and responsibilities! Then when Mum did find out he upped and left without so much as a word of apology. To hear him talk it was my mum's fault for putting on a bit of weight and not wanting to go out much to the sort of posh places he likes. Anyway, he was droning on about his problems and how hard up he was and all the time, I was clutching my stomach and thinking to myself, I'll stop him. I'll stop him dead in his tracks. I'll tell him about the baby.'

'But you didn't?'

'Didn't get a chance,' said Zoë. 'One minute he's on about his tax bill and the next minute he's dropping a bombshell of his own. Lorraine's pregnant, he said. Lorraine's his partner, see?'

Karen saw. Saw before Zoë explained further, how that might change things.

'Mum went wild,' said Zoë. 'She's a lot like me, you know. Puts things off till she absolutely has to face them. I reckon that all this time she's been expecting him to come back. That he'd get sick of Lorraine or, more likely, that she'd get sick of him. But with the kid on the way, Mum had to face it. It was permanent. They're even getting married. That was when Mum really flipped. Suddenly there's stuff flying round my bedroom. Slippers, chair, jug of water, the lot.'

'Oh heck!' said Karen, unable to imagine a row of those proportions.

'It was quite funny really,' said Zoë. 'My dad was so made up with the idea of fatherhood again that he hardly seemed to notice. Ducked now and again to avoid the missiles and all the time with this stupid glow on his face. I didn't know whether to laugh or cry. In the end I dived for cover under the bedclothes and waited for it to calm down a bit.'

'And did it?'

'Yeah. I knew it would. Mum runs out of steam eventually. Or out of things to throw! And then my dad picked up exactly where he'd left off. Explaining how he'd got to be more careful with his money now the baby was on the way. And I wanted to yell out, what about me? What about my baby? But I sort of knew he wasn't going be too thrilled about being a dad and a grandad all at the same time.'

'So you kept quiet?'

Zoë nodded.

'Not because of Dad,' she said slowly. 'In the end, I kept my mouth shut 'cos of Mum. After all the shouting and chucking things around, she went dead quiet. And real pale. She never moved for about ten minutes after he'd gone. Then she just said she'd got a migraine and she was going for a lie down. So I was stuck there, on my own, with the pains coming more often and I hadn't a clue what I was going to do.'

'Why didn't you phone a doctor or me or anyone – someone?'

'I don't know,' said Zoë. 'I just sort of lay there, in a daze, waiting to see what would happen. Nothing did. Not for ages. I even got up and made Mum a cup of tea.'

'And she still didn't notice there was anything odd? That's not possible,' said Karen. 'It's just not possible.'

'She hardly noticed I was there, let alone what I looked like,' said Zoë. 'I've been putting on these baggy sweaters over my nightdress to prowl around in, so she didn't notice any extra bulges. Not that there was much, as you know. An' the bug accounted for me looking a bit out of sorts. So there we are.'

'Not quite,' said Karen. 'You still haven't explained how you managed to give birth on your own, without her so much as noticing.'

A thought occurred to Karen, in the brief silence that followed.

'This is true, isn't it, Zoë? This isn't another game. Telling me what you think I want to hear?'

Zoë smiled.

'Strange but true,' she said.

Karen believed her. But barely. Here was Zoë talking about giving birth to a child, with no hint of emotion. No tears. Only a placid smile of almost total detachment.

'Anyway,' said Zoë, 'Mum took some sleeping pills

with her tea. And what with them and the stuff she'd taken for her migraine, I knew I was on my own. I wasn't too worried, really. The pains had sort of stopped, so I went back to bed. It was gone nine by that time and I was absolutely wiped out. Then, in the early hours of Monday morning, I wake up and it happens. Just like that. Don't say it, Karen! Don't tell me those gruesome stories about your Auntie Pat having to have an epidural or that friend of your mum and her Caesarian. All I can say is it wasn't like that for me. One minute I've got a nasty stomach cramp and the next minute I've got a baby.'

'It's unbelievable,' said Karen.

'Yeah,' said Zoë. 'Funny, isn't it? The one time in years I decide to tell the truth and it's more incredible than all my lies put together.'

'And then what?' said Karen. 'What did you do? How did you *feel*, for heaven's sake?'

'I don't think I felt anything. It was weird. I just knew what to do. As though I'd been through it all in a previous life or something.'

'More likely the result of all those films the school nurse brought in,' said Karen. 'But even so, it's incredible. There's no way I could have—'

'Probably not,' said Zoë. 'But you don't know what you can do until you have to. So there I was. I cut the umbilical cord, got the baby cleaned up and I wrapped him in an old blanket. And I stand there holding him and looking at him, waiting for something. Some feeling. Some great gush of mother love to pour out. But it doesn't. It's like he's got nothing to do with me at all. Oh, for heaven's sake, Karen!'

Zoë passed over a box of tissues.

'You're a right softie, you are.'

'We're talking about a baby,' Karen managed to mumble through her tears. 'Your baby, Zoë. And you sit there calmly saying you don't want anything to do with him.'

'That's not what I said,' Zoë snapped. 'It wasn't like that. It was more like he didn't want anything to do with me.'

'Don't be ridiculous!'

'And why should he? I thought,' said Zoë, ignoring Karen's interruption. 'Who'd want to be landed with a mother like me?'

'Very neat,' said Karen, her tears evaporating in the heat of anger. 'Turn it round. Justify what you did, if it helps.'

'Don't go all saintly on me, please. You don't know what you'd do in the same position. I didn't! I mean, I didn't plan it all out, you know. I didn't think, right, I'll have the baby and leave it on a doorstep.'

'So what did you think?'

'That's the point. I hadn't thought about it at all. So when he started to cry, I panicked. No, not panic. It was like I was acting on automatic pilot. There was this thought in the back of my head. No one need ever know. He'd arrived so quietly. So easily. All I had to do was—'

'Get rid of him?'

'Don't make out like I murdered him or something, Karen. I was real careful. I lined the box with newspapers.

Made sure he was warm and everything. I even waited till it was almost light, so someone'd find him straight away.'

Big deal, Karen wanted to say. What a heroine! What a thoughtful mother. But she held it all back. Waiting. Waiting for Zoë to show some sign of regret, responsibility, some indication that she cared.

'You know the rest, really. I left him outside the medical centre. Came home. Had a bit of a dodgy moment 'cos Mum had surfaced and asked me where I'd been. Told her I'd puked up and needed some fresh air. Good move that, 'cos it also explained why I shoved the bedclothes in the wash and why I wasn't fit to go to school. So that was it.'

'Not quite,' said Karen. 'Didn't you wonder what had happened? Didn't you care?'

''Course I did,' said Zoë. 'I've had the radio and telly goin' all day, every day. I'd seen it all a dozen times before you phoned. But I had to pretend I hadn't. 'Cos I knew what you'd think. I was cursing myself for ever having told you. If it wasn't for that—'

'You'd have got away with it. You'd have left him, wouldn't you? Left him and never looked back.'

'I don't know. I've been thinking about him.'

'Sure.'

'I know what you think of me, Karen. And I don't blame you. And I wouldn't blame you if you never believed another word I said. But I want you to believe this, right? I've thought about him every bloody minute. Every second of every day. And when you walked in here and said you'd seen him, I wanted to kill you. Because it should have been me. I should have gone. I wanted to. But I couldn't.'

Karen didn't believe it. It simply didn't ring true, this sudden remorse. This change of heart. But how could you ever tell with Zoë? Who could say what went on inside her mind?

'So what now?' said Karen, utterly drained.

'Now you're going to help me.'

Chapter 10

'OK,' said Karen, knowing she had to take advantage of this sudden remorseful mood before it changed again. 'I'll help you. The first thing we've got to do is tell your mother, right?'

'Right,' said Zoë, getting out of bed and starting to dress. 'We'll go down and tell her then, eh? You can say—'

'No way,' said Karen. 'I'm coming with you for support, that's all. You tell her.'

As it happened, neither of them could tell her. She wasn't there. She'd left a note on the table to say she'd had to pop to the shops for extra fish fingers.

'Well, she shouldn't be long,' said Karen.

'Depends who she gets talking to,' said Zoë. 'She could be gone for hours.'

Zoë started to pace up and down. Karen feared she would lose her nerve, change her mind, if her mother didn't turn up soon.

'Look,' Zoë said, echoing Karen's fears. 'I can't stand this waiting around. I need to do something. Now. Why don't we phone that hot line number they've been giving out?'

'Good idea,' said Karen. 'I've got it written down.'

'So have I,' said Zoë. 'Don't even need to look, actually. I know it off by heart. I nearly phoned after the very first news I saw. Honest I did! But, oh, come on. Let's get on with it.'

She picked up the phone and dialled the number. Karen heard it ring out. Heard somebody answer, though she couldn't tell what they said. There was barely time before Zoë slammed the receiver back down.

'I can't. I'm sorry, Karen. I just can't.'

'All right,' said Karen. 'We'll wait for your mum.'

'No,' said Zoë. 'You don't understand. I can't tell anyone. I can't face it. I don't want to.'

'Tough,' Karen snapped. 'You don't have a choice now.'

'What'll happen?' said Zoë, suddenly looking no more than a child herself. 'What will they do? They might prosecute. They might send me to prison. You can't let that happen to me. You can't.'

'I don't think it will,' said Karen. 'Honest, I don't. They'll be pleased you've come forward. They won't prosecute but they'll want you to get help. See a counsellor. That sort of thing. To help you sort out what's best for you and Steven.'

'But why?' said Zoë. 'Why put myself through all that? Why not just let it go? Please, Karen. Let's not say any-thing. What's the point of ruining my life? Mum's life?'

'What about his life?' said Karen.

'He'll be all right,' said Zoë urgently. 'You know he will. There are people out there desperate for babies. Someone'll adopt him. Love him to bits probably.'

'And when he gets older?' said Karen. 'What then? What about when it's time to tell him he's adopted?'

'Do they have to do that?'

''Course they do,' said Karen.

'Well, it's no big deal,' said Zoë. 'Lots of kids are adopted.'

'Sure,' said Karen. 'But at least most of them know something about their background. Who their natural parents were. Why they couldn't look after them. That sort of thing. Imagine not ever knowing. Imagine being told that you were dumped on a doorstep in a crisp box! Think about it, Zoë.'

'I'm sure his adoptive parents could explain. Put it to him carefully. And as long as he'd been happy with them, I can't see as it would matter too much.'

'Oh can't you?' said Karen. 'Then maybe I should spell it out for you.'

This was it, then. Choice time. One option was to just walk out of here. Go home. Pick up the phone, tell the police about Zoë and leave it all up to the authorities.

The other option was to try to make Zoë do it herself. To make her see it was for the best. But the only way she was ever going to do that was by playing her final card. By telling her own secret. Her own story.

'Spell what out?' Zoë was saying.

'I'm going to tell you something, right?' said Karen. 'Something I've never told anyone before. Something I don't want anyone else to know. So you don't repeat it. You don't tell anyone at school. You don't tell Tracy or your mum or anyone else.'

'OK. Get on with it. I won't tell nobody.'

'Promise.'

'I promise.'

'You said you thought it wouldn't matter, didn't you? You said as long as Steven was happy with his adoptive parents, he wouldn't care what sort of box he was found in or who might have left him there.'

'Yeah. I reckon.'

'Well, that's not true.'

'Is that it? Is that your big revelation?'

'Sort of. Because I know, Zoë. I know just how he might feel. Because it's how I feel. My parents, the people I live with, my adoptive parents, are great.'

'You're adopted?' said Zoë incredulously. 'Is that what you're telling me?'

'Yeah,' said Karen. 'I'm adopted. And my parents love me to bits, as you put it. And I love them.'

'Well you seem happy enough,' said Zoë. 'Most of the time. In your own dull sort of way.'

'Yes. I'm happy enough.'

'So, that's what I said. It'll be the same for him. He'll be happy enough too. He'll be with people who really want him.'

'I haven't finished,' said Karen. 'I'm happy enough most of the time because I don't think about it. Don't talk about it. Block it out. But then, something happens. I see something, read something, hear something and it all comes back. This emptiness of not knowing who I am or where I came from. And I think, what sort of person was she? My mother. Why did she leave me and never look back?'

'Let me get this straight,' said Zoë. 'You're not just

telling me you're adopted. You're saying you were left? Abandoned? Like I left Steven?'

'Almost. Not quite the same. I was older. About three months. And my mother, whoever she was, didn't leave me on the steps of a medical centre. Or on anyone's step. She left me in a public toilet. In a park. In Manchester. And that's all I know about my origins, my background. I don't know where I was born or who my birth parents were. I don't even know for sure that it was my mother who left me. It could have been anyone. Father. Grandmother. Neighbour. Nanny or careless babysitter.

'I don't know what my name was or whether anybody gave me a name before I was Karen. I don't even know exactly when I was born. My birthday's made up. A good guess by the doctor who happened to be on duty when someone found me and took me to hospital. Apparently I was in a bit of a state. Whoever had been taking care of me hadn't done a very good job of it. Perhaps that's why they dumped me. But the point is, Zoë, I don't know. I'll never know. And however hard you try, however hard your adoptive parents try, that's a hell of a gap to live with.'

Karen had barely looked at Zoë while she was speaking. She looked now, waiting for a reaction. She was shocked when it came. She'd been expecting all manner of things. But not this. Zoë was laughing. Actually laughing.

'Aw, come on, Karen,' Zoë said. 'I know what you're trying to do but you can't play me at my own game. How long did it take you to make that lot up?'

'Make it up!' Karen screamed. 'Are you mad? I

94

haven't made anything up. It's true. Every single flaming word of it.'

'But that's incredible!'

'An incredible coincidence, maybe. That's why I could barely believe it when I saw the news about Steven. I never thought I'd know anybody, meet anybody, in circumstances anything like mine. But then to end up with a friend who did what you did. To have to live it all over. That's why I had to see him. That's why I had to go that day. It was like trying to look at myself.'

'No,' said Zoë. 'Stop it. I don't believe it. It's not true. For heaven's sake, Karen, what sort of idiot do you take me for? I've seen your parents. Both of them. You even look like them. I mean, call me a racist if you like but you can hardly help noticing, can you? I mean, your mum's white. Your dad's black and you're sort of in between. And it's not only a colour thing. You talk like your mum. You act like her. The funny way you tilt your head to one side when you're listening. She does that. So how the heck can you stand there telling me you're adopted?'

'I don't know why I'm doing this,' said Karen. 'I don't know why I'm even trying to explain this to you, because, at the end of the day, I don't think it will make the slightest difference. You'll still go on in your own selfish way. Believing what you want to believe, doing what you want to do. What's best for Zoë. But I'm not going to let you hide from it. This is the truth and you're going to face it just like I have to do. Like Steven will have to.

'I look like my parents because the social workers try to plan it that way. If the baby is obviously Asian they find an Asian family. If it's mixed race, like me, then that's what they look for. I was lucky. Mixed race matches can be hard to find, so they tell me. But I was placed pretty quickly. And as for acting like Mum, sounding like her, that's learnt, isn't it? You don't live with someone for fourteen years without picking up some of their ways.'

'Possibly,' said Zoë thoughtfully.

'Come on,' said Karen.

'What are you doing?' said Zoë, as Karen grabbed her arm. 'Where are we going?'

'I'm going home and you're coming with me. Leave a note for your mum.'

'Why? Why should I?'

'Because I've got something you need to see, to help you make up your mind.'

They knelt on the floor of Karen's bedroom as Karen pulled a large photograph album out of the drawer under her bed.

'Right,' she said. 'Family album time. Only when you're an abandoned baby they don't call them that. They call them Life Story Books.'

She opened the album and showed the title.

'So that's the first thing you need to know. This is what Steven will have. They'll have started it already. Taking photographs of him. Photographs of the nurses who look after him. Photographs of the person who found him. So when he's older, his parents can point and say, look, there's the nice man who found you. In my case it was a lady, see.'

Karen pointed to a picture of an elderly woman.

'There she is. Mrs Pringle. Mrs Pringle who happened to be caught short whilst taking her dog for a walk in the park. Ties the dog up. I've even got a picture of the dog, look! Mrs Pringle leaves the dog, goes into the loo and finds a baby. We exchange Christmas cards every year, me and Mrs Pringle. She's eighty-six now. Unfortunately, Mrs Pringle didn't have a camera with her, so someone had to go back later and take pictures of the park and the toilet. You can see why I don't make a habit of doing this, can't you? I say, would you like to see a photograph of the loo I was found in, isn't the best way to impress your friends, is it?'

'You don't have to be ashamed of it,' said Zoë quietly. 'It's not your fault.'

'No. But can you imagine what people would say? At school and stuff. People like you and Tracy who got at Shaheen for being Asian or Gemma for being fat. Think what fun you could have with someone who was found in a loo or a crisp box!'

'That's different.'

'Yeah, it's different. And that's what bullies go for, isn't it? People who are different. But we haven't finished yet. You haven't seen the pictures of the nurses. This one's Karen. That's who I got my name from. They named

Steven after the guy who found him, didn't they? Lucky they didn't do that to me. Mrs Pringle's called Gertrude. Can't see myself as a Gertie, somehow. Then, of course, there's the social workers. Steven's bound to have some pictures of Miss Hobbs already to put in his book.'

She turned over a page.

'There's my social worker, look. Shane Gallagher. I don't remember him, of course, but I've got his picture. Can you imagine what it's like at school? When they ask you to write those essays about yourself? Bring your photographs in. My nice, ordinary ones start at thirteen months when I was adopted.'

'I thought you said you were only three months when you were found.'

'I was. But they don't hand you over to someone straight away. They wait to see if anybody claims you. Whether anybody notices they might have accidentally left their baby in the loo. Whether somebody's friends and family happen to notice a three-month-old baby has disappeared. In my case they didn't. Can you imagine that? Three months old and nobody missed me. Or, if they did, they didn't let on.

'And then there's all the paperwork. Finding the right family. It can take years in some cases. I was lucky. But when it comes to family album time, there's no way I'm going to show this round the class, is there?'

She moved up close to Zoë before speaking again.

'Is that what you want? Is that what you want for Steven, Zoë? A Life Story Book that doesn't even begin

98

to tell him anything? A family album without a single picture of you, or your mum? Pictures of a crisp box and a social worker. Pictures he won't ever want to show anybody? Is it? Because if it is, I'll close the book and you can go home and I promise I'll never say another word. I won't ever tell anybody. Think about it, Zoë. It's your decision.'

Chapter 11

Zoë flipped over the pages of the book.

'You were telling the truth,' she said quietly.

'I usually do,' said Karen. 'Except for the small matter of my origins. I never even mention I'm adopted unless I have to. Saves any tricky questions, see?'

'It's awful,' said Zoë even more quietly. 'I'm sorry, Karen.'

'Don't be,' said Karen. 'Not for me. You're not responsible for that.'

'No, but like you said: what you must have been through these last few months. And when you saw him, on telly and in the hospital! I never thought. I never guessed.'

'Why should you?'

'I never asked, did I? I never asked anything about you. I just envied you with your boring little life. Your two parents, living together. It all looked so safe and cosy.'

'It is,' said Karen. 'Most of the time. And don't get me wrong. I love my parents. I really do. I can't imagine ever being with anyone else. Or wanting to be. I'm not even sure I'd like to meet my birth parents, even if I could. All I really want is to know. I want to know who they were and what they were like. But I never will and Steven won't either.'

'He will,' said Zoë. 'We're going to do it. We're going to do it now.'

★

Karen lay on the settee, her mother sitting beside her, her father in the chair opposite. It was gone midnight and they were all exhausted but sleep was out of the question.

So much had happened in the last few hours. Karen's parents had been the first to hear the story. They had sat and listened to Zoë calmly relating her tale as tears spilled down Karen's face.

They had driven the girls to Zoë's, where the story unfolded again, with certain omissions. Zoë had been reminded over and over of her promise. She would not tell Karen's secret. Would only say that Karen had helped her make up her mind to claim her baby. Never reveal just how she had done that.

'Oh, my poor Zoë,' was the reaction of Zoë's mum. The same words repeated over and over. Punctuated only by: 'Why didn't you tell me? Why didn't you tell me, love?'

Karen had thought that her role was over then. But no. Zoë wanted her around. Wanted her to wait until they'd phoned her dad. Wanted her to stay until he arrived, gaunt and pale. She had heard the recriminations, both parents blaming the other.

'How could you not have noticed? She's living with you, for heaven's sake. You're not fit to be called a mother!'

'I may not be fit but at least I'm here for her, which is more than you've ever been! What sort of example did you set her? You and your affairs!'

Fruitless, pointless accusations which went on until the

101

police arrived. Two officers – a man and a lady – who sat, impassive, taking down the details as calmly as Zoë told them.

They had insisted on phoning an ambulance, despite Zoë's protests that she was fine and the offer, by her dad, to drive her to hospital.

At that point Karen had felt sure she could make her escape. There wasn't room in the ambulance for crowds of people. Her parents would take her home. But again, no. Zoë had insisted. Had refused to go without Karen. Had actually screamed and cried, when Karen tried to leave. In the end, it was Karen who travelled in the ambulance with her, both sets of parents following in cars with a police escort.

'Like something on telly,' Zoë had said.

More like being trapped, Karen had thought, in a room with the walls slowly closing in. She was already further than she wanted to go, more deeply involved than she wanted to be. She had feared she would never escape, never again be allowed out of Zoë's sight.

It was Steven who saved her. After what seemed like an age of waiting while Zoë was admitted and settled into bed, they brought the child. Karen had wanted to hold him, touch him. But it was Zoë's arms they placed him in.

A scene as peaceful and beautiful as any painting. Except for the crying. Karen's crying. A wail of agony that Zoë barely noticed.

'You'd better take her home,' a bewildered nurse had said to Karen's parents.

At the door, Karen had paused. Gone back. Knelt by Zoë's bed. Whispered something.

'It's OK,' Zoë had answered. 'Stop worrying. I promised, didn't I? Come and see us tomorrow, eh?'

Karen looked at the clock on the mantelpiece. It was already Thursday and she'd be in no fit state to see Zoë or go to school.

'I think she's drifted off,' she heard her mother say, as a blanket was draped over her.

'No,' said Karen. 'I'd just closed my eyes. I was thinking, that's all.'

'I wish you'd told us,' her mother said. 'I wish you'd told us earlier.'

'I've explained all that.'

'I know. And I'm not getting at you. I just wish we could have helped, that's all. I wish we could help now.'

'You are helping,' said Karen, trying to smile. 'You always do. It's just that, well, you know. I try not to...I try not to care but it's brought it all back. Showing Zoë those pictures.'

'I'm really proud of you,' her dad said. 'It was so brave. To put yourself through all that. I only hope Zoë appreciates it. I hope she understands what it meant to you.'

'I think she does.'

'I hope so,' he said again thoughtfully. 'And I hope she keeps it to herself. I know how hurt you'd be if it got out.'

'It won't,' said Karen. 'I know Zoë's a bit on the selfish side, but she won't tell anyone. She promised.'

It was gone three when Karen finally got to bed, gone

103

midday when she surfaced again. Too late to go into school. Her mother was getting worried.

'I know you've been through a lot but you can't afford to miss school. Your work's been going off a bit, these last few months. Not surprising, considering! But it's not that long till your exams.'

'I know,' said Karen. 'But it's not that bad. Honest. I can catch up. Shaheen and Paula will help. I'll go back on Monday.'

'Tomorrow.'

'Tomorrow's Friday. There's hardly any point.'

'There certainly is,' her mother insisted. 'Oh, by the way, Zoë phoned. She was expecting you at the hospital this morning. Just how selfish can that girl get? I told her you'd been up half the night.'

'I'll go now.'

'Not now. I'll give you a lift on my way to work this afternoon. But then, that's it. No more time off. And you should tell Zoë you can only see her at weekends from now on.'

Karen nodded as her mother's lecture continued. She didn't tell her she'd already decided to phase out her friendship with Zoë. She'd done all that she could.

As Karen arrived at the ward, someone was just leaving. A young man carrying a heavy-looking black case.

'Who was that?'

'Oh, just a photographer,' said Zoë.

'Photographer?'

'Come to take pictures of me and Steven. For the local paper.'

'Is that a good idea?'

'I dunno. Don't see why not. Everyone round here will find out soon. And other people'll want to know. There's loads of 'em been following the story, he says.'

'Yes, but I thought you'd want it kept anonymous. Just mother reunited with baby. No names. Let alone your picture splashed all over the place.'

'Mum said it was all right. She had to give her permission 'cos I'm under sixteen. Couldn't see the point of covering it up. Not now.'

'Well I hope it doesn't cause bother, that's all,' said Karen, angry that Zoë seemed to be lapping up the attention.

'What sort of bother?' said Zoë, in genuine innocence.

'People asking questions, that's what,' said Karen. 'I mean, journalists can wheedle things out of you. What if they start asking about the father? What then?'

'Then I don't tell 'em. I say that's my business. I mean, if I spill the beans he'll be in right trouble, won't he? Me under sixteen and everything.'

'Have you heard from him?'

'No, why should I?'

'Well it's his baby too.'

'You're forgetting, Karen. The father doesn't even know about it.'

'It's you that's forgetting. I talked to Tracy, remember? She told me the whole story about what happened that day. How you burst in there and confronted him with it. I just thought he might have checked. Might have cared.'

'You don't half talk in riddles,' said Zoë, laughing. 'What are you on about now?'

'Mr Parsons.'

'Mr Parsons!' Zoë screeched. 'Mr Parsons!'

'Sssh, the nurse is looking.'

'I'm sorry,' said Zoë, wiping tears of laughter from her face. 'But you've got a right knack of getting the wrong end of the stick, as it were. I mean, you're saying you think that jerk is the father of my baby?'

'Isn't he?'

'No, he certainly isn't! Honestly, what d'you take me for? Or him for that matter? He was a bit of a drip, I grant you, but hardly the type to mess with his pupils.'

'That wasn't what you said when you got him sacked for allegedly messing with Tracy.'

'He resigned, Karen. He panicked and resigned, that's all.'

'But why? If he hadn't done anything to Tracy, or you? Why did he have to go?'

''Cos he'd made a mistake, that's all,' said Zoë. 'That field trip we went on. Well, me and Tracy got involved with some older lads from another school, yeah?'

'Yes. Shaheen and Paula told me.'

'Well, I got a bit more involved with my lad than Tracy did with hers. Or I was a bit more careless. In more ways than one. I never meant nothing to happen. I wasn't prepared. It all went further than I meant it to. It was an accident.'

106

Karen looked at little Steven, as Zoë described the incident in every detail. An accident. His arrival in the world the result of a moment's carelessness. No love involved. Barely any passion either, if Zoë were to be believed. A casual encounter.

Were those her own origins? Was she an accident? A mistake? Did it matter any more? Had it ever really mattered?

'Anyway,' said Zoë, 'Mr Parsons found us in a compromising position, as they say. So what should he have done?'

She carried on before Karen had a chance to answer.

'He should have told a senior teacher, that's what. Got me sent home. Informed my parents. Got me to a doctor for one of them check-ups, in case I'd caught something or needed one of them morning after pills.'

'So why didn't he?'

''Cos he's a right softie, that's why. I threw a wobbler. Pleaded with him. Told him it wasn't as bad as it looked. That we hadn't actually gone the whole way. That my dad would kill me if he found out. All that rot. So he kept quiet. Nice but not very professional, see?'

'OK,' said Karen. 'But why didn't you do something when you got home? If you knew you might be pregnant?'

'Karen, don't be thick. You don't get pregnant every time, you know. Some people try for years to have a baby. How was I to know I was so unlucky?'

'Unlucky?' said Karen. 'All those talks we get, leaflets

we're given, videos we see! Didn't you take any notice? Didn't you think about contraceptives? Didn't you even consider pregnancy or Aids?'

'Sure I thought about it,' said Zoë. 'A bit. But Aids, getting pregnant, they're things that happen to other people. Or so I told myself. People who have loads of partners. And I hadn't. He was only the third!'

Karen shook her head. Zoë was so careless. So casual about everything. So impossible to understand.

'So,' said Zoë, 'getting back to our friend Mr Parsons. That day when I was drunk and told him I was pregnant, he was right shocked. Knew he was sort of responsible, see? Professional misconduct for not telling at the time. He went white and Tracy jumped to the same conclusion you did. Started yelling at him, calling him a pervert or something. Then she sort of launched herself at him. That's when he hit her.'

'Hit her?'

'Well, hit her, pushed her, whatever. I don't think he meant to hurt her, just get her off him. But, as you know, she grabbed him as she fell and that's when someone walked in. You can imagine how it looked.'

'Yes,' said Karen, trying to make sense of it, 'but why didn't you tell the Head the truth? There and then? Mr Parsons had tried to help you, for heaven's sake and you repaid him by getting him sacked.'

'He'd have had to go, whatever we said. He'd covered up the original business and hit Tracy, hadn't he? That'd be enough to finish him. Especially when everyone knew he was such a lousy teacher anyway. We did him a favour, really. I honestly think he was glad to go with as few questions as possible.'

'But if you'd never gone in there! Never mentioned being pregnant.'

'I didn't mean to,' said Zoë, shrugging. 'I've told you over and over. I was drunk. I didn't think.'

'You never do, do you?'

Chapter 12

'Oh, give it a break, Karen,' Zoë snapped. 'I never claimed to be no saint, did I? You're worse than the nurses and that counsellor I've got to see. She was here this morning before I'd even had the chance to wake up, asking a load of stupid questions. Trying to get me to tell her who the father was.'

She looked down at Steven and laughed.

'Well,' she said more seriously, 'I've reformed. I'm not going to let this muck up anybody else's life. I told her it was none of her business. My mum knows what you know. Time and place but no names.'

'Isn't she interested? Doesn't she care?'

'Not especially,' said Zoë, shrugging. 'Why should she? What does it matter? We'll just put father unknown on the birth certificate.'

'And what if the father reads the paper? Sees your picture?'

'You think he'll remember me, do you? I'm probably one of dozens!' she said casually.

'Let's say he does remember.'

'Karen, he probably won't even see the paper! It's not as if he's local. And if he does, why on earth should he assume he's the father? I told him I had a boyfriend at home, for a start.'

More lies. Did Zoë lie to everyone she came in contact with?

'And if he does even consider he might be the father,' said Zoë, 'well, it'd be up to him, wouldn't it? It might make him squirm for a bit, wondering if I'll tell, but if he's got any sense, he'll keep quiet. I mean, I *am* under age. Technically he committed a crime.'

'And you don't think he has a right to know?'

'No. I certainly don't!' said Zoë. 'It's not as though we're going to get married and live happily ever after, is it? I barely know the lad! And I'm quite happy to be a single mum.'

'Mum?' said Karen. 'Does that mean you've decided against adoption? You're going to keep him?'

'May as well,' said Zoë, as if discussing a dress she'd got from mail order. 'Me and Mum had a talk about it. Dad too. They both agreed I should keep him. Mum's really made up with him, actually. It's given her a whole new interest in life. And to be honest, Karen, I couldn't give him up now. I mean, look at him! He's absolutely gorgeous. Who could give up—?'

'A baby?' said Karen. 'People do.'

'I'm sorry.'

'It's OK. But I just think you should be sure. Give yourself a bit more time. Look at all the implications. Make sure you can really cope. Bringing up babies isn't a game, Zoë. I mean, make sure he's not just a novelty that you'll tire of in a month or two, when he's being sick and screaming through the night. 'Cos if that's going to happen—'

'Give it a break, Karen! You sound like one of them

111

RSPCA adverts! Not just for Christmas and all that,' said Zoë, laughing. 'Oh, don't go all huffy on me! I have thought about it. Honest. And I am sure. Me and Steven are going to be fine.'

'So how are you going to manage? For money and stuff? I mean, your mum struggles as it is and with your dad's problems . . . That's another good reason to contact the father. Shouldn't he pay something towards the upbringing? You won't find it easy.'

'Karen,' said Zoë, 'I know worrying's a full-time job with you, but you can worry about something else now, OK? I've told you. Me and Steven are going to be OK. And as for money, I've got something worked out. You'll see.'

Karen didn't find out exactly what that was. The nurse came round at that point to weigh Steven and give Zoë some pills for her blood, which was lacking iron, apparently. Shortly afterwards Zoë's mum had appeared and Karen had taken the opportunity to leave. She said she'd call again soon but doubted if she would. Not for a while, anyway.

She'd promised her parents that she'd try to settle back into school. Catch up with her work. Not that it would be easy, at first. The story made front page of the paper on Thursday night and was the sole topic of conversation at school on Friday. Karen pretended to be as surprised as everyone else. It was easier that way. The newspaper article hadn't mentioned her at all. Why should it? It simply said that after days of agonizing, Zoë had decided to claim her baby.

'I can't believe it,' Paula said. 'Pregnant. All that time she was hanging round with us and we never even noticed. Mind you, if her own mother never knew...'

'I reckon she must have done,' said Shaheen. 'I wouldn't be surprised if she'd encouraged her to dump it in the first place. You all right, Karen? You're shaking.'

'I was shaking when I first read it,' said Paula. 'I wanted to go round there and hit her. Fancy leaving it in a box. Anything could have happened. A dog could have attacked it. Some nutter could have picked it up. I mean, what sort of person is she? How could anyone do that?'

'Don't,' said Karen. 'Please don't. You don't know, do you? You don't know what you'd do, if you were desperate.'

'I'd never be that desperate. Not to dump a defenceless baby. Well, at least she came forward, I suppose. That's something. You get some who never bother.'

'Shut up!' Karen screamed.

'What's wrong? I only said—'

They had the attention of everybody in the playground now. Everyone who'd been having their own conversations about it, putting forward their own views. 'Well don't!' Karen screamed at her again. 'Shut up! Shut up, all of you. You don't know anything about it.'

Karen had apologized later in the day, when she'd calmed down. Her friends had been upset, confused, but they'd accepted the apology.

'I don't know why I blew up like that,' said Karen. 'I

113

haven't been sleeping much. Bit of bother at home. Mum and Dad going through a bad patch.'

She didn't know why she'd said it. It wasn't true. But she had to say something, make some excuse.

'Yeah,' said Paula. 'I know what you mean. I have the same problem.'

'Your parents not getting on?' said Shaheen sympathetically.

'Oh, no. My parents are fine. It's my next-door neighbours. Yelling at each other half the flaming night. No one in our road gets any sleep.'

Karen had smiled. The tension was diffused, at least for the time being. If she could just get through another week or so, it would all blow over. Someone would get expelled. There'd be a fight. Something else to talk about.

At least that's what she told herself over the weekend. A quiet weekend, spent at home, trying to pull herself together. There was only one minor interruption to her recovery, early on Saturday morning when the phone rang. She heard her mother answering, curt and anxious.

'No. It's nothing to do with us. I'm sorry. I don't want to talk about it and I'm certainly not letting you talk to my daughter.'

'Who was that?' Karen had asked.

'It's unbelievable,' her mother had muttered angrily. 'That Zoë is just unbelievable. She's been talking to a national paper now. One of the Sunday tabloids. You can just imagine the sickly headline, can't you? Honestly, you'd think she was some kind of heroine!'

'Yes, but why did they phone us?'

'They wanted us to confirm the story, apparently. I told them to get lost. Well, you heard most of it.'

'That means she's mentioned me. To a newspaper! You don't think, oh, Mum, you don't think she's told them?'

'No, calm down,' her mother said. 'I'm sure she hasn't told them any details. Not about your background. They just knew you'd been at the hospital with Zoë, when she claimed him. That's all.'

'I don't know,' said Karen. 'I'm not sure. That doesn't ring true. I'm going to phone her.'

Karen phoned the hospital. Got the reassurance she wanted. Yes, Zoë had spoken to the national paper. Yes, she might have mentioned Karen's name. But no, she hadn't told them any details. She was sure of that.

Karen vaguely wondered what she *had* told them, how much of it would be the truth. But as it wasn't a paper Karen's family bought, she'd probably never know. Didn't want to know. With any luck Zoë would never come back to school. Their brief friendship would be over. Karen could try to forget and concentrate on rebuilding her relationship with Paula and Shaheen.

With that in mind, she arrived early on Monday morning. She was always early for school but that day particularly so. She wanted to see Paula. Have time to talk. Make sure everything really was OK after her stupid outburst on Friday.

Paula wasn't there. Nor was Shaheen. But there were others. Kids from her year. From other years. Nobody she knew particularly well but ones who would usually say 'hi', at least. Yet they were all carefully avoiding her. Turning their heads as she passed, pretending they hadn't even seen her. Not in a nasty way. Not quite. It was as though something had happened. Like she'd contracted some contagious disease or a close relative had died and they didn't know what to say; as though they were embarrassed about something.

A couple of girls wandered across, whispering. They looked as though they were about to join her, then suddenly thought better of it and veered away.

It was weird. She wasn't imagining it. She wasn't being paranoid. She looked down at herself to see if she was wearing odd shoes or her pyjamas or something. But everything seemed in order. She looked exactly as she always did.

She was still looking, still checking, when Shaheen and Paula arrived. Unlike the others, they headed straight for her. Paula was clutching a newspaper. One of the popular Sunday tabloids. The one that had phoned on Saturday. The one Zoë had spoken to.

'Have you seen this?' Paula asked.

Karen's stomach dropped to her toes. Paula's tone. The look on her face. The embarrassed reaction of everyone in the playground. What on earth had Zoë told the paper?

'Give me that,' Karen said, more sharply than she intended.

Paula opened up the paper. Turned to one of the inside pages. Folded it back. Karen breathed a sigh of relief, as a picture of a model flashed into view. Very sophisticated. Very seductive. Slim. Blonde. The face of the decade. Tracy? That's what they were showing her. Nothing to do with her. Nothing to do with Zoë. Just Tracy. But no. Before she had a chance to examine it properly, to decide whether it really was Tracy, the paper was being turned over. It was the other page she was supposed to be looking at. The one with the massive headline, impossible to ignore.

'SECRET AGONY OF DUMP MUM'S FRIEND.'

'I'm sorry,' said Paula. 'All that garbage I came out with on Friday. What must you have thought? I didn't know. I had no idea. Why didn't you tell us, Karen? We'd have—'

'Shut up,' said Shaheen. 'I've told you, Paula. She didn't tell us because it isn't true. You know what a liar Zoë is. She's made it up. I know she has. Karen wouldn't be stupid enough to tell Zoë anything that sensitive, whatever the circumstances. My dad says Karen ought to sue.'

Paula's words, Shaheen's words, their faces, the newspaper – all converged in one massive blur. A thick cloud looming towards Karen, wrapping itself round her, tightening, choking, making it impossible to breathe. Her friends grabbed her before she fell. Steered her to a bench. Forced her to sit down.

'Come on, Karen,' Paula urged. 'Take some deep breaths.'

'I'll get Mrs Wilson,' said Shaheen.

'No,' Karen managed to whisper. 'Not yet. I'll be all right. Honest.'

She gripped the edge of the bench. Breathed deeply, as

Paula instructed. Waited for her eyes to focus again. By the time they did, a crowd had gathered at a barely discreet distance. Their embarrassment almost gone, they were now hovering, eager to know whatever details the paper had missed out.

'Get lost,' Shaheen screamed at them. 'Leave her alone. It's not a spectator sport.'

'It is, though, isn't it?' said Karen. 'How much did she tell them? What does it say? Read it to me.'

'I can't,' said Paula, passing the paper to Shaheen.

'Are you sure?' said Shaheen.

'Oh yes,' said Karen. 'I'm sure. Read it. Every word.'

Chapter 13

Karen tightened her grip on the bench as Shaheen started to read, in a voice so quiet she was barely audible.

'"The teenage mum who dumped her day-old baby reclaimed him last week after being shamed by her best friend. Zoë, fifteen, revealed to us that her friend, Karen, won her round by recounting that she, too, had been abandoned as a baby. *I never knew about Karen's background,* Zoë told us. *It was an amazing coincidence. She guessed I might be Steven's mum, and she kept badgering me until I broke down and admitted it. I still didn't have the guts to claim him until Karen told me that she'd been abandoned in a public toilet, in a Manchester park, when she was about three months old. She was found by an elderly lady and named after one of the nurses who cared for her. I was staggered. Imagine how I felt when I found out."'*

'Oh, yeah,' Karen snapped. 'How *she* felt. Typical, that is. What about how I felt? How I feel? She's told them everything.'

Her voice trailed off. She felt Paula's hand gently touch her shoulder, as Shaheen read on.

'"*Karen pleaded with me not to put my baby through what she'd been through. Not to make him live with the pain of never knowing. After that,* Zoë told us, *I had no choice. I told Mum, who was great about it all and before I knew what was happening, I was there, at the hospital, holding my baby in my*

119

*arms. It was wonderful. I knew I'd done the right thing, at last.
I don't care what happens now. Having my baby back is all that
matters."'*

'Oh, puke,' said Paula. 'How can newspapers print that
drivel? All that gush about getting her baby back. As if she
cares about the baby or Karen or anyone else for that
matter. How could they be so stupid? How could they be
taken in?'

'I was,' said Karen. 'I knew her better than anyone and
I trusted her.'

'You're freezing,' said Paula, touching her white hand.
'Let's get you home.'

'No. Not yet. Read the rest, Shaheen.'

'"Zoë hit the headlines on Friday,"' Shaheen began,
'"when she showed up and admitted being the young
mum who had dumped baby Steven in a box outside a
Leeds medical centre. But, until she spoke to us, no one
knew what had made her change her mind.

'"Karen, the secret heroine of the saga which touched
the nation, was staying mum last night. Her mother
refused to let us speak to her but the story has been
confirmed through other sources."'

'The nerve,' Karen screamed. 'The bloody nerve of it!
They didn't say when they phoned. Mum just thought
they wanted us to say something about Zoë claiming
Steven. And Zoë lied to me again. How could she do
that? She promised. She promised.'

Shaheen handed the paper to Paula.

'So it's all true?' said Paula, in total bewilderment.

120

'What Zoë said, you were—'

'Yeah, it's true. Not exactly the sort of thing you're proud of, but it's true. And I've never told anybody. Not unless it was someone official, someone who absolutely needed to know. And now Zoë's told everybody.'

'But why on earth did you tell Zoë?' said Shaheen. 'Why trust her with something like that? Zoë of all people.'

'Because of Steven,' said Karen. 'Because I needed to make her understand. I thought I had. I thought she did. But she couldn't have done. She's told everyone. The whole bloody world knows now.'

'It doesn't make—' Paula began.

'Don't tell me it doesn't matter,' Karen screamed. 'Don't tell me it doesn't make any difference. Look at them. Look at them all whispering and pointing. That's Karen. She was found in a loo, you know. How would you feel, Paula?'

'I don't know,' said Paula. 'I'm sorry—'

'Don't be,' said Karen. 'It's not you who needs to be sorry. It's her. Look, I'm going. I'm going to see her now. Tell Mrs Wilson . . . something . . . anything. Show her the bloody paper!'

'You can't go on your own,' Shaheen said. 'You look terrible. You're in a right state. Let me come with you.'

'No.'

'Well, can I at least phone your mum? Tell her what's happened? Where you're going?'

'Do what you like,' said Karen. 'It doesn't matter now.'

★

121

Zoë was sitting on the edge of the bed when Karen arrived, surrounded by a pile of envelopes, wrapping paper, baby clothes, rattles and cuddly toys. Like the booty from a game show.

'Well wishers,' said Zoë, holding up a blue rabbit. 'Loads of people have written and sent stuff. People I don't even know.'

'Great,' said Karen. 'Marvellous. Read about it in the newspapers, did they?'

'Do I take it you've seen it then?' said Zoë, producing the offending article from her bedside table.

'Dead right, I have. About an hour ago. In the playground. At school.'

'Whoops.'

'Whoops? Is that all you can say? Have you any idea what it was like?'

'Well, I can see that might have been a bit upsetting. With an audience and all that. I thought you'd have had the sense to buy one yesterday.'

'Do you think that would have helped? Do you think it would have mattered when and how I saw it? Today, yesterday, tomorrow. What difference would it make? And why the hell should I have bought it? I phoned you on Saturday. You promised you hadn't let on. You promised!'

'Yeah, well, I got a bit confused. Forgot exactly what I'd said.'

'Forgot? You forgot you'd broken your promise? Forgot you'd told them what I pleaded with you not to tell?'

122

'You said yourself, Karen. Journalists wheedle things out of you. Claiming my baby was old news, in a way. They were looking for a new angle. I had to give them something for their money.'

'Money? They paid you? You sold me out? Literally? This is all another pack of lies, isn't it?' said Karen, suddenly catching on. 'They didn't approach you, did they? You approached them. They didn't trick you. You did it quite deliberately. You lousy, hypocritical, lying b—'

'Calm down, for heaven's sake. I can't see what you're making such a big deal about. Nobody's going to care, Karen. In a couple of days it'll all be blown over. Forgotten.'

'I care.'

'That's 'cos you get too emotional about things. Think about it rationally, for once. I might even have done you a favour.'

'Favour?' Karen hissed.

'Getting it out in the open, instead of brooding and bottling it all up, for a start. It's not good for you. No wonder you're so uptight all the time. You need to get it out of your system. Talk about it more.'

'Since when do you know so much about it?'

'That counsellor I'm seeing. She says it's good to talk about things.'

'I don't think she meant to a newspaper though, did she?'

'Who knows?' said Zoë, in her casual way. 'The article might even jog someone's memory, conscience or whatever.'

'Conscience? How would you know anything about conscience?'

'It's not big on my agenda, I admit. But don't you see, Karen? It might help. You said you wanted to know about your background. Well, now someone might come forward.'

'And I'm supposed to be happy about that, am I? Well, I'm not.'

'Why the sudden change?'

'I'll tell you why, Zoë. For years I've wanted to know. I've spent hours looking in the mirror, trying to see my mother, somewhere in me. Trying to imagine what she was like. I've examined all my good points. All my bad points. Working out which were inherited, which were learnt. Trying to piece together a picture. And I chose what I wanted to see. Someone who loved me. Someone who might have been poor, sick, unbalanced, desperate, but someone who cared. Someone who tried to give me a better life in the only way she could.'

'Yeah, well, that's probably right.'

'That's what I always managed to believe, Zoë. That's what Mum and Dad encouraged me to believe. That my birth mum loved me. That she was, somehow, OK. But I can't hide behind that any more, can I? That fairy tale. That fantasy. Because now I know the truth.'

'I'm not exactly following,' said Zoë.

'No, you wouldn't. What I'm saying is that I don't ever want to know her or meet her now. And do you know why? Because now I'm scared she'd be just like you. And

124

I'd hate her. Do you hear me, Zoë? I'd hate her.'

'Hear you? Half the flaming ward can hear you. Honestly, I don't know what you're getting so worked up about.'

'No, you don't, do you? You're not even sorry, are you? Not for any of it. Not for me, not for Mr Parsons, not for Steven—'

'By the way,' said Zoë wearily. 'It's Liam. I've decided to call him Liam Steven and if you don't pipe down, you're going wake him up.'

'I won't wake him,' said Karen. 'I'm going.'

Sitting on her bedroom floor, Karen wondered how she'd managed to get home. She vaguely remembered leaving the hospital, sitting on a bus, her head throbbing and her stomach churning so violently she'd had to get off several stops before home. She supposed she must have walked the rest of the way.

She remembered ringing the bell. Fumbling for her key when no one answered. Pushing open the front door and heading straight for the kitchen. Pouring a glass of water and rummaging in the medicine cupboard until she found some paracetamol. She had taken the bottle to the bedroom, swallowed two tablets and waited for the machine guns in her head to stop firing. When they didn't, she had taken two more. How long ago was that? Half an hour?

Too soon to take any more but the guns were still blazing. Looking at the Life Story Book probably wasn't helping. But she couldn't stop turning the pages. None of this for Liam Steven now. At least some good had come out of this mess. Or had it? She might have spared him the Life Story Book, the agony of never knowing. But what had she inflicted on him instead? And at what cost?

She was seeing a photograph of a run-down, red brick public toilet, covered in graffiti. She was hearing the whispers of the playground. Her hands were reaching out for the bottle of tablets, knowing that she couldn't face the whispers again. It would be easy. How many would you have to take to be sure? To sink into oblivion. Never having to wake. She pressed the top of the bottle before unscrewing it. Childproof. But she wasn't a child any more. She wasn't going to swallow them in mistake for sweets. She knew what she was doing.

The face of Mrs Pringle stared out from another photograph.

'Don't look at me like that!' she said, slamming the album shut. 'It's my life! It's nothing to do with you.'

But, in a way, it was. If Mrs Pringle hadn't found her, her parents had once said, if she'd been left another hour, it might have been too late.

Everything that had happened since, everything that was Karen, was the result of Mrs Pringle's weak bladder.

Karen felt a weak smile creep, unwanted, to her lips, as her hands played with the open bottle.

She heard her name being called, was aware of the door opening.

'Karen!' her mother shouted. 'Oh, thank goodness. I

went to the hospital after Shaheen phoned. I must have just missed you. Zoë didn't seem to know where you'd gone. I made her give me the newspaper. I couldn't believe it. I was terrified you wouldn't come straight home. Karen, what are you doing with those?'

'Putting the top back on,' said Karen. 'And please don't shout. I've got a headache. That's what the tablets are for.'

Her mother put the newspaper down and snatched the bottle. Held it up. Seemed momentarily calmed by the amount left.

'Are you sure? You weren't going to—'

'No,' said Karen, starting to cry as she felt her mother's arms tighten around her. 'I don't think I was.'

'We'll go away,' said her mother. 'Take a holiday. Get you out of circulation for a bit.'

'I don't think so,' said Karen. 'I'd still have to face it when I got back. I'd rather face it now. I'll go back to school tomorrow. I'll manage, somehow.'

'I know you will. You always do.'

'I managed before by hiding it away. But I can't do that now, can I? Everybody knows I'm just some poor little waif that somebody didn't want.'

'No, you're not! You're Karen. And we want you. We love you. And so do your friends. It's you they care about, love. Not your background. Not your origins. None of this really makes any difference.'

'That's what Paula tried to say.'

'She was right. It can only hurt you if you let it. Maybe having to face it all like this might even help in the end.'

'You sound like Zoë! She said that. Made out she'd done it to help me! And the funny thing was, I think she believed it. I've realized that Zoë's lies aren't lies at all. Not to her. She lives in a complete fantasy world. One where her actions are never selfish. Where she never has to face up to her responsibilities.'

'Maybe she'll have to, now she's got the baby.'

'I doubt it. I mean, she's fine at the moment. Revelling in all the attention. But what happens when the novelty wears off? When she gets bored? When she realizes what having a baby is all about? What sort of life will Liam Steven have then?'

'Who can say, love? That's up to Zoë. And her family. You never know, having someone else to think about, rather than herself, might be good for Zoë.'

'Zoë! Oh, I'm sure Zoë will be all right. She'll make sure of that. But what about the rest of us? Me, Liam Steven? Was it worth it, Mum? Did I do the right thing? Did I?'

'Yes, you did,' said her mother firmly. 'Whatever happens you did the right thing. You couldn't have stood by and done nothing, could you? You'd have had it on your conscience for the rest of your life.'

Karen nodded and allowed her mother to hold her, soothe her, comfort her, as she always did, until the phone rang and her mother reluctantly went off to answer it.

While she was out of the room, Karen's eyes were drawn back to her Life Story Book and the newspaper. She opened the book, before picking up the article. Reading it again. Over and over.

'That was your dad on the phone,' said Karen's mother when she returned. 'He's seen the paper! He's absolutely furious with them. Thinks we should sue or contact the Press Complaints Commission or—'

'No,' said Karen. 'Don't let him do that. It would mean more hassle. Dragging it out. I don't want that. I want to move on with my life.'

It was true. It was time to look at the present, the future, not the past. In the future there was hope. She would go back to school, cope with the gossip, catch up with her work, pass her exams, maybe go to university.

In the future she had her family, her friends, her ambitions. In the past there was only pain. It was time to let go. It wouldn't be easy. She knew that. It had never been easy. It wasn't easy now. Not with the Life Story Book still spread out on the floor and the article still resting on her knees. It was time to put it all away. She folded the article, put it between two pages of her book and closed it.

But as she did so, she couldn't help remembering what Zoë had said about conscience. Couldn't help wondering... was there someone out there, reading that paper, thinking of her?

Epilogue

Sally Wentworth looked at the phone and poured herself another drink. She'd been drinking all morning, since dropping the kids at school. Drinking like she hadn't done for a long time.

She picked up the empty bottle, wrapped it in newspaper and put it in the dustbin. She didn't want Paul to see it. Or the kids. It wasn't going to become a habit again, she told herself. Just today. Just to get her through today.

She slumped at the kitchen table and stared at the pieces of newspaper she'd kept. One from yesterday, the other from fourteen years ago, retrieved from its hiding place in a wallet wedged under a pipe which ran behind a bedroom cupboard. Two jig-saw pieces forming a picture of a time before Paul. Before she was respectable Mrs Wentworth. When she was just fifteen. About the same age as those girls in the paper yesterday. Zoë and Karen.

Only Karen wasn't really Karen. Hadn't always been Karen. She was Michelle. There was no doubt about it. Sally stood up, moving uncertainly towards the window of the neat semi, staring into the garden with its flowers in pretty borders and a swing for the kids to play on.

She'd come a long way since the damp, tiny flat in Birmingham which she'd shared with her sister, Julie, and later, of course, with Michelle.

Julie was three years older than her. The flat was rented

in her name. Sally had taken refuge there. It was temporary at first. Odd nights or weekends when things were unbearable at home. Then, after that last, massive row with her stepfather, she had simply quit going to school, moved in with Julie and neither of them had seen the rest of their family from that time on.

Mum had never bothered trying to contact them. Never knew about Michelle or the four grandchildren that had come along since. Never cared what had happened to her... or to Julie.

Michelle hadn't been born in the flat. She was born in hospital. Hadn't stayed in the flat long either. They'd moved when the baby was just a month old. To another flat in another city. Manchester. To get away from the snoopers, the health visitor and social worker.

'We don't need them,' Julie had said. 'Believe me, Sal. They'll take her away, if we're not careful. I know they will. They're always bleating on about summat. She's underweight. Her nose is running. She's wet. You haven't changed her. The flat's damp. I wouldn't mind if they did owt. Got us a decent place. But they won't. They'll just have her taken into care.'

It was possible. The social worker didn't like Julie. Thought she was a bad influence. Didn't like the idea of Sally being left with her, let alone a baby. But Julie wasn't too bad. They had a good laugh together, got on fine. They were doing OK with Michelle too, until Karl moved in.

Not that you could blame Karl for everything, Sally

thought, as she opened a new bottle and poured herself another drink. Looking back, she could see she and Julie had been a mess. Drinking heavily. Doing drugs sometimes. Not a lot. They'd never really had the money for it. But Karl was a dealer. It was different after Julie took up with him. After Julie started on heroin.

And Karl hated Michelle. Couldn't stand her crying. Went mad if Julie went near her.

'Let Sal do it,' he'd snarl. 'Get her out of here, Sal. I want her out of my sight, OK?'

And Julie had stood by, watching it happen. Too besotted with Karl, too drugged up to see what was going on, to care about what was happening to Michelle. The poor kid was losing weight. She was dirty most of the time and covered in sores.

'I did my best,' Sally told herself, over and over. 'I was only a kid. I did my best.'

But it had been impossible, stuck there in that flat with no money of her own. Everything had deteriorated so fast. She'd known she'd have to break free somehow. She'd tried. She'd really tried. She'd got herself a job in a café. It had been a worry leaving Michelle with those two but she desperately needed to save some money. It came to a head that night she came home early. Julie and Karl were yelling at each other. Michelle was screaming, lying on the bed where she'd been dumped.

'I want rid of her,' Karl shouted. 'And yer betta do something fast before I do.'

'No!' Sally had yelled, as Karl moved towards the bed.

He'd picked Michelle up, started shaking her...

Sally put her fist in her mouth to stop herself screaming at the memories. Memories of herself trying to tear the baby away, while Julie looked on with glazed eyes, unable or unwilling to help. Memories of Karl eventually giving up, virtually throwing the baby at her. Sally had clutched Michelle and left the flat, walking the streets until the early hours until she'd thought it was safe.

She'd gone back, thrown her things in a bag and planned to leave the next morning. She'd hoped that she'd be able to persuade Julie. That Julie would go too. Her, Julie and Michelle together. She'd planned to take the baby to a doctor, to try and get help.

But in the morning, Michelle had gone.

'What have you done?' she'd screamed at Julie. 'What have you done with her?'

'She's safe. Quit fussing.'

'If he's hurt her—'

'He hasn't,' Julie drawled. 'But he might. So it's best this way.'

'Oh, no... I don't know what you've done but I'm not letting you get away with it!'

'You're not letting me?' Julie had yelled. 'And what do you think you've got to do with anything, Sal? Michelle's my kid. It's my decision.'

Sally hadn't been able to argue with that. Michelle was undoubtedly Julie's child, even though it had always been Sally who had cared the most. Who had tried to look after Michelle.

'Karl says he won't put up with some other bloke's kid,' Julie had insisted. 'And why should he? So you just keep out of it, little sister. 'Cos I wouldn't want you to get hurt or nothing.'

Was that what had kept her quiet? Sally thought, getting up from the table and staring out of the window again. Fear of Karl?

Maybe. For the first few hours, she'd been too terrified to move or speak, certain that the baby was dead. Equally certain that her threats had been empty. She couldn't go to the police. Couldn't let anything happen to Julie.

Later, when Karl had appeared and thrown the newspaper at them, Sally had been more relieved than anything. A three-month-old baby had been found in a park, close to their home. Nurses had called her Karen.

There had been no point after that. No point saying anything. Michelle/Karen was best off where she was. And besides, Julie had disappeared. Left with Karl, the night after dumping the baby.

She'd done the right thing, Sally told herself, as she gripped the window-sill to stop her hands shaking. She had her own life to lead. Then and now.

She'd done all right for herself. Moving to a flat above the café where she'd worked. Saving a bit of money. Meeting Paul that day he'd called in the café and politely complained that his coffee was cold.

Paul had made the difference, Sally reflected. He was real straight, was Paul. Worked hard. Hated drugs. Had even got her to quit smoking when she was pregnant

134

with the first of their kids. She'd sort of reinvented herself for Paul. She'd told him very little about the past. And half of that had been lies. He loved kids, did Paul. He could never have understood about Michelle.

There had been a dodgy time, about six years ago, when Julie had tracked her down. Turned up on the doorstep, penniless, desperate and very sick. They'd both ended up in hospital: Julie for an operation and herself, later, because the upset over Julie had set her off drinking again.

Paul had been brilliant. He'd borrowed money to send her to a clinic. Luckily, it had worked. She'd promised Paul it would never happen again. And it hadn't. Not until today.

A knot tightened in her stomach as she turned and saw the paper lying on the table. The paper that had brought it all back.

What was she supposed to do? Phone the paper? The social services? Tell the secret she had kept for fourteen years? Reveal herself to her niece? And if she did? Then Paul would find out. Her kids would get dragged into it. They'd find out just what sort of person their mummy used to be. The very thought made her retch.

But on the other hand, how could she just ignore it? Wasn't this fate's way of making her put right the past? Didn't Michelle have a right to know?

'"Don't put your baby through what I went through,"' she read aloud. '"Don't make him live with the pain of never knowing."'

Sally's hand stretched out towards the phone and then fell limply at her side. What good would it do? Surely she'd only be stirring up people's comfortable lives for no reason. What could she really tell Michelle? She couldn't give any information about the birth father. Julie had never told her who the father had been. She didn't possess any certificates. Any proof. Only memories of two hopeless kids.

Agonizing memories were all she had to pass on. It wasn't as if Michelle could ever know her natural mother. Poor Julie had died in that operating theatre six years ago. A drug addict. Her mind and body totally wrecked. That was the news she had for Michelle. That her mother was a junkie, her father unknown, her aunt too selfish to care. Was that what Michelle wanted to hear? Or was she best left being Karen?

She was a real nice kid, by the sound of it.

Sally picked up the paper. Her eyes blurred, reading the story one last time. Pity there was no picture of Karen. Only Zoë and the baby. It would be nice to know what Michelle looked like now. Whether anything of Julie was still alive in her.

So many things to think about. Her head was pounding with the impossible decision she had to make. To tell or not to tell.

If only she'd never seen the paper. If only the article had never appeared. Sally's eyes focused on a single word. Zoë.

Zoë, whoever she was, had a lot to answer for.

More Fiction for you to enjoy

FACE
TO
FACE
Sandra Glover

Haunted. The word sprang into Naomi's mind. That was the word she'd been looking for when she'd been talking to Stella and Anna about Adelle.

Adelle is the new girl at school. She rejects offers of friendship and stands alone in the school playground, her shoulders hunched as if carrying the burden of a terrible secret. As Naomi wins Adelle's friendship, she begins to realise Adelle's problems are like no other she has encountered, especially after Adelle's told her about the face in the mirror.

'A powerful ghost story for our own time.'
Independent

ISBN 184270012X £9.99

More Fiction for you to enjoy

CRAZY GAMES

SANDRA GLOVER

'What you doing, Col?' Brad had asked.
'Sharpening this,' Colford had answered as if sitting around,
in a World War 1 uniform, sharpening a piece of wood with a
rather evil-looking knife, was perfectly reasonable behaviour.

The last thing Brad wants to encourage is the
friendship of Colford Rattersby, a strange boy who
talks to statues and who seems to live in a fantasy
world because the real one is so awful.
But, despite having plenty of problems of his own,
not least his relationship with fiery Stacey, Brad gets
drawn into Colford's increasingly bizarre behaviour
and the games which are starting to drift from
harmless fantasy towards dangerous reality . . .

ISBN 1842700669 £9.99